"With searing honesty, deep inte[...] ticity, Stacey Padrick grapples with the often difficult, yet mysteriously grace-filled realities of everyday life and everyday faith. She shares her hard-won wisdom with openness, grace, and wit, proving that wisdom and faith-filled living come to those who embrace life with a gracious heart, a seeking spirit, and an ever-deepening faith."

—Jean M. Blomquist
Author of *Wrestling Until Dawn*

"Stacey Padrick has a bright, positive, and warmly Christian approach to a large theme. She draws in the reader from the first line and holds on to both our minds and hearts throughout. I am pleased to highly recommend Stacey Padrick and her book."

—Earl F. Palmer
Senior Pastor, University Presbyterian Church of Seattle

"Stacey Padrick gently draws us beyond the idea that God is there to answer our prayers and bless our plans. She shows how the losses and limitations we most fear can actually be avenues to the deep experience of God that our hearts long for. *Living With Mystery* challenged me to look at the hard things in life from God's perspective and gave me tools to discover God's heart for myself."

—Susan Maycinik Nikaido
Senior Editor, *Discipleship Journal*

"Stacey Padrick's writing is inviting and engaging. Drawing on a rich variety of sources—Scripture, devotional classics by Christians of all stripes, and her own experiences—she takes the reader to a safe, hospitable place where the deep questions of disappointment and faith are examined honestly and fearlessly. Ultimately, Stacey's frank vulnerability and words of encouragement inspire her readers to take comfort in life's journey with all its twists and turns, confident in the deep love and graciousness of God. Her book is one to which readers will return again and again for insight and inspiration."

—J. Brent Bill
Professor, Earlham School of Religion

LIVING

WITH

MYSTERY

STACEY PADRICK

BETHANYHOUSE
Minneapolis, Minnesota

Published by Bethany House Publishers
A Ministry of Bethany Fellowship International
11400 Hampshire Avenue South
Bloomington, Minnesota 55438
www.bethanyhouse.com

Printed in the United States of America by
Bethany Press International, Bloomington, Minnesota 55438

Library of Congress Cataloging-in-Publication Data

Padrick, Stacey.
    Living with mystery : finding God in the midst of unanswered questions / Stacey Padrick.
        p.   cm.
Includes bibliographical references.
    ISBN 0-7642-2439-5 (pbk.)
    1. Christian life. I. Title.
BV4501.3 .P33   2001
248.4—dc21
                                                                    2001001318

To my parents,
whose love, example, and encouragement
have helped me to embrace life
in all its mystery.

With utmost admiration and appreciation,
Stacey

STACEY PADRICK is a free-lance writer, speaker, and business-woman from San Francisco. She received her B.A. in Business, and her M.A. in International Relations while attending graduate school in England as a Rotary scholar.

Stacey is well published in periodicals such as *Discipleship Journal, Today's Christian Woman, Current Thoughts and Trends, Woman's Touch*; devotionals such as the *Upper Room*; as well as in newspapers such as the *San Jose Mercury News*.

She speaks at women's retreats, fellowship groups, churches, and professional clubs. Her passion is inspiring believers to pursue deeper intimacy with God and to walk boldly by faith.

A woman who loves adventure, she has traveled to twenty countries, lived and worked on three continents, loved and lost, risked, wrestled with chronic illness, grown, hoped, and embraced the many mysteries of walking by faith.

Please visit her Web site at *www.staceypadrick.com*.

ACKNOWLEDGMENTS

I am so very grateful to those who contributed to the making of this book:

My sister, *Sheri*, who stood beside me while I wrestled with many of these mysteries, who first instilled in me a desire to learn from the wisdom of others (thanks for all those quotes you copied for me!), and who gave me my first book about growing in faith. *Steve Laube*, who caught my vision, enlarged it, and championed it from proposal to press. Thanks for believing in and caring for me not only as a Bethany author but also as an individual. To *Christopher*, whose editorial expertise and calm spirit made the revision process easy. To *Nancy*, who graciously made those last minute changes!

To all those who influenced and encouraged me as I first embarked on my writing career: *Jean Blomquist*—friend, mentor, and inspiration—whose gentle encouragement and helpful editing guided me forward. You are an answer to my prayers. *Elaine Colvin*, whose practical teaching and contagious enthusiasm inspired me to pursue publication. *Dr. Margaret Baker*,

Elaine Kurtovich, Glyn Nordstrom, and others who were moved by my letters and suggested I consider writing as a career.

The editors (*Sue, Adam, Susan*) at *Discipleship Journal* for publishing my articles and continually encouraging me about my writing. Special thanks to *Susan Nikaido,* the first editor to tell me: "I think you really have talent"—giving me courage to pursue what I felt called, but very unqualified, to do.

The *Elton Trueblood Academy* and *Earlham School of Religion* for awarding me a writing fellowship, the use of Elton Trueblood's personal library in which to write this book, and especially, the help of Professor *Brent Bill,* an invaluable writing coach, counselor, and friend.

I deeply thank my prayer supporters, cheerleaders, and dear friends without whom I would not have completed this: *Desirée Hodson* (especially your visits, feedback, humor, and prayers!); *Susan Reed* (your enthusiasm about my proposal made me believe this was worth pursuing!); *Jamie Lisea* (your listening heart and wisdom); *Amy Nelson* ("you and Max!"); *Dave Garr* (master of google.com); *Brenda Quinn* (thanks for all your prayers and pep talks over e-mail); *Judy Gann* (whose perseverance in the face of lupus inspired me); *Linda Cherne* (whose laugh kept me going even on those foggy SF days); *Jill Peterson* (for your visit, milkshake run, and prayers during that final stretch); *Stacy* (your letter revived the Hope chapter I'd almost tossed in the trash); *Mary T., Julia, Jen, Michele, Tamara, Sharon, JK, MaryBeth, Alison, Elizabeth, Simone & Harvey, Simon & Becky, Barbara A., Aunt Bernice, Hugh, Sibylla, Barbara H., Mary L., Dru Scott* . . .and all those who have shared with me, laughed with me, wondered with me, prayed with me—you have influenced my life and thus this book.

Suzi Dillon, who first discipled me as a new believer and continued praying for and cheering me on ever since. My professors at Westmont College, particularly *Dr. Shirley Mullen,* who encouraged me to ask questions I could not answer. My grandmother, whose prayers for my salvation and physical healing have sustained me. *Rev. Fred Harrell*, who teaches me every Sunday what it means to live the gospel.

Special thanks to *Eric*, whose life richly blesses mine with laughter and love. I choose us.

Finally, I would like to thank my *First Love*, whom I pray this book pleases and honors most.

CONTENTS

INTRODUCTION

You are so young, so before all beginning, and I want to beg you, as much as I can, dear sir, to be patient toward all that is unsolved in your heart and try to love the questions themselves like locked rooms and like books that are written in a foreign tongue. Do not now seek the answers, which cannot be given you because you would not be able to live them. And the point is, to live everything. Live the questions now. Perhaps you will then gradually, without noticing it, live along some distant day into the answer.

Rainer Maria Rilke,
Letters to a Young Poet

AS THE YOUNGEST MEMBER in my family, when we all gathered together on my parents' bed to watch a mystery on Friday-night TV, I never quite understood all that was happening in the plot. I didn't understand much, for that matter, but oh, how I wanted to.

"What does that mean?" "Where is she going?" "Is he going to die?" I would ask.

After responding to my first few queries, family members began replying with shorter answers and increasing tones of impatience. By my fourth "What's happening?" I finally got the "*Ssshhh!* No more questions!"

As a young child I was often told, "You're very curious!" It's still true. I like questions. I like to ask and wonder and seek. And as a child, I assumed every question had an answer that could be found.

As I grew older I learned this wasn't always the case. When I went to college, my inquiries became broader and deeper. Only after studying under brilliant professors, whom I expected to have all the answers, would I realize that no one did. Some questions never could be answered—at least not in this finite world with our limited minds. Fortunately my professors still encouraged me to ask, to wonder, to seek.

In time my penchant for digging to unearth answers to all my questions evolved into an appreciation for the questions themselves. I found value in the wrestling. Instead of fearing mysteries I couldn't solve, I learned to *embrace* and *live* them.

LIVING THE MYSTERY

The *Oxford Dictionary* defines mystery as "a religious truth that is beyond human powers to understand." We base our lives upon spiritual truths beyond our understanding. *The first shall be last. In giving, we receive. In dying, we live. In weakness, we are strong.* We don't wait to live these biblical mysteries until we fully grasp them. Rather, we live them by faith—upside down as they may seem—and only then can we truly begin to comprehend them. To live the mystery is to embrace life in the midst of unanswered questions. To live the mystery is to embrace the questions themselves as stones that pave—not obstruct—the path toward deeper intimacy with God.

Limitations. Love. Brokenness. Desire. Darkness. Hope. Risk. We all face these mysteries at some point in our lives. When they test our faith in God, we're tempted to resort to superficial solutions, simplistic answers, or short-cut remedies. We think that because Jesus is the Answer, we must have all the answers—about pain, suffering, loss, disappointment.

However, God does not call us to a life of following answers and formulas. He calls us to a life of following *Him*. Rather than waiting for answers to lead us closer to God, we can better know Him here and now in the midst of our questions. God waits for us not in some distant, far-off answer down the road, but here, in the intersection of uncertainty. This book will help us embrace the questions and struggles in our lives as mysteries to be *lived*. And as we live them, just maybe we'll find we come to know God, others, and ourselves more deeply.

Chapters 1 through 5 address the challenges and opportunities we face while living with uncertainty; chapters 6 through 7 introduce unexpected ways to fuel our relationship with God; and chapters 8 through 10 share the hope and joy we can experience even in the "not knowing."

I have written *Living With Mystery* not as someone who has solved these dilemmas, but as someone who's experienced God's faithful presence while living them. In each chapter, I offer not answers but clues along the road of life's mysteries.

As we venture on the journey of faith—with no promise of answers, only the promise of God's presence—we find that these very mysteries reveal to us a depth of God we have not previously known . . . or perhaps even imagined. My prayer is that through this book you will come to know God more deeply and more intimately as you *live the mystery.*

CHAPTER REFLECTIONS

At the end of each chapter, additional resources will help you reflect, either alone or in a group, upon what you have read. The reflections, which vary somewhat from chapter to chapter, will help you discern what God may be revealing to you about himself and yourself through these mysteries.

QUESTIONS FOR JOURNAL AND/OR SMALL GROUP

These are designed to help you apply what you are discovering. They can be used individually as journal questions, in a small-group setting, or as ideas to discuss with a friend.

VERSES TO TREASURE

Although many verses could apply to each chapter topic, I have chosen those that most spoke to me as I have grappled with each mystery. Scripture, in addition to God's grace and the prayers of loved ones, kept me standing when my knees wobbled like Jell-O. We cannot overestimate the incredible power of God's Word to sustain us when circumstances weigh us down and to clear our vision when tears cloud our eyes. His Word will not return void without accomplishing what He desires in your life. Cling to it as you would to a sword in battle.

Meditating upon the Word of God transforms our thoughts and attitudes. I encourage you to take time to practice scriptural meditation. A good start is to set aside five minutes during your devotional time. As you take a few deep breaths, quiet your mind from any distractions, internal dialogue, or even talking to

God. Slowly repeat the verse as you breathe. If a word or phrase strikes you, take time to repeat it and allow the Spirit to speak to you through it. Ask God to silence all voices that are not His and to speak to you through His Word.[1]

Relish the verse or passage like your favorite dessert. "How sweet are Thy words to my taste! Yes, sweeter than honey to my mouth!" (Psalm 119:103).

When a verse especially speaks to me, I like to write it on the back of a business card or file card and keep it with me in my purse or Day-Timer. Then, when I'm standing in line at the post office, sitting in traffic, holding on the phone, or taking time out for a break, I can practice memorizing it. "Thy word I have treasured in my heart, that I may not sin against Thee" (Psalm 119:11).

THOUGHTS FOR CONTEMPLATION

I have selected quotations—some shorter, some longer—to spark further reflection on each chapter topic. Many of the authors I cite throughout the book have been like ropes to me during the most challenging peaks of life I've climbed. Clinging to their wisdom, words, and stories of God's faithfulness, I've found my balance steadied even when the howling winds of life's troubles have threatened to blow me off the rock. I trust they will also bless and minister to you.

PRAYER

Reading others' prayers can help us pray when we're having difficulty formulating our own words. This section includes prayers from various authors as well as some of my own.

GUIDED MEDITATION

This section will help you interact with a passage of Scripture through meditation. Allow yourself at least fifteen minutes for this exercise, and keep a journal handy in case you want to record your thoughts and anything you sense God might be showing you.

HYMNS

Classic hymns contain rich teaching, truths, and pearls of wisdom from those who have gone before us. Sing to the tune if you know it. Otherwise, make up your own melody as you go along. Or simply read the song meditatively. Each hymn relates specifically to each chapter topic.

ADDITIONAL RESOURCES

For further growth and challenge, I have included supplemental resources (readings for reflection, prayer guidance, poetry, practical helps, and other addendum material) after the epilogue. Enjoy!

But we speak the wisdom of God in a mystery,
the hidden wisdom, which God ordained
before the ages for our glory.

—1 Corinthians 2:7 NKJV

1

HIDE-AND-SEEK:

THE MYSTERY OF HONESTY

O Lord, thou has searched me and known me. Thou dost know when I sit down and when I rise up; Thou dost understand my thoughts from afar. Thou dost scrutinize my path and my lying down, and art intimately acquainted with all my ways. . . . My frame was not hidden from Thee, when I was made in secret, and skillfully wrought in the depths of the earth. . . . Search me, O God, and know my heart.

King David,
Psalm 139:1–3, 15, 23

Why do you say . . . "My way is hidden from the Lord?" . . . His understanding is inscrutable.

Isaiah 40:27–28

HIDE-AND-SEEK

Anthropologists studying societies throughout the world have discovered that children of all cultures engage in some variation of hide-and-seek.[1] Ever since the first man and woman, we've been a people who love to hide.

I still keenly recall the thrill and anticipation at age six of running to the living room and slithering behind the curtains while my sister counted *"One, two, three. . . ."* When I heard *"Ready or not, here I come!"* my little spirit surged with tense hope to not be "exposed"—while simultaneously yearning eagerly to be found. The game was no fun if the seeker couldn't locate the one missing. Children want to be found—but *first* they want to be sought.

We still play these games as adults. We gravitate toward concealing our true selves behind curtains of pretense, images, and masks. Yet we long to have someone seek to discover who we really are, someone who will call us out from hiding. Though we elude the One seeking us, our hearts sink with disappointment if we are ultimately not found. Shrouding our real, our deepest, selves from God and others, we play spiritual hide-and-seek.

The first step to living the mystery begins with honesty—with ourselves, with others, and with God. Because He knows our tendency to hide, the all-seeing God calls us out. He pursues us.

"Where are you?" He beckoned to Adam and Eve. Though He knew exactly where they were concealed behind bushes in the Garden, He wanted them to reveal themselves.

"Where are you?" He beckons to me, as I veil myself behind the appearances of piety or perfectionism I assume are more acceptable to Him than the real me. As God sought for Adam and Eve to emerge, so He whispers to me daily: *"Come out from behind the curtains. Reveal yourself to me. Let me know you."*

COMING OUT OF HIDING BEFORE GOD

"Behold, I stand at the door and knock; if anyone hears My voice and opens the door, I will come in to him, and will dine with him, and he with Me" (Revelation 3:20).

In St. Paul's Cathedral in London, a famous portrait by Holman Hunt beautifully illustrates this verse: Jesus knocks at the symbolic portal of a human heart, waiting for an answer. Looking closely, the viewer of the painting observes there is no knob on the outside, where Jesus stands. Only the one being beckoned, not the one beckoning, can open the door.

So it is with our hearts. God wants to know me—the deepest parts of me—but will never force himself inside. He knocks. He calls. He waits. Yet ultimately He leaves the decision to open the door up to me. Will I open it? Will I let God really know me?

In the French language, two different verbs describe "to know": *savoir*—to know something as a fact (such as "I know that she lives on Franklin Street"); and *connaitre*—to be familiar with, to know personally and experientially (such as "I know *her*, inside and out"). Though God sees everything about us, He wants to know (*connaitre*) us intimately. Thus He knocks, asks, and calls to draw us out.

How much of myself will I reveal to Him? Only what I think He'll find acceptable? Or will I invite Him into even the back closet—that corner of my heart where I conceal those secret feelings of envy and pride, selfish habits of keeping the best for myself, negative thoughts of self-pity and self-defeat? When God called Adam, he replied, "I heard you in the garden, and I was afraid because I was naked; so I hid" (Genesis 3:10). Just as

Adam's shame at his nakedness drove him to hide, my fear of exposing my shortcomings and failure tempt me to run and hide behind the bushes, hoping that somehow I might elude the Lord's all-seeing eye.

Yet even as God calls us to reveal ourselves, "no creature [is] hidden from His sight, but all things are open and laid bare [before] Him" (Hebrews 4:13). What sweet release comes under His gaze. He knows it! He sees it! Before a word is on my tongue or a sin is in my heart, He knows it all (Psalm 69:5). This truth draws me out of hiding, for nothing is truly concealed from His view. As much as I run to elude God, my heart, playing hide-and-seek, longs to be exposed, longs to be set free from the darkness of sin and shadows, longs to be drawn into His presence.

Nothing quite exposed my heart like the year I taught at a university in China. Adjusting to a cultural and political system very different from what I had always known, my life felt placed upon a glass slide. Being pushed under the microscope of living overseas—testing me in ways I had never been tested before—and living with someone from whom I could not hide revealed unhealthy bacteria in my heart.

Teaching the same classes of students that my roommate and dear friend, Desirée, taught exposed my competitiveness when the students began comparing us. If they seemed to like her more, the bacteria of jealousy surfaced. When they praised my teaching—pride. When our coveted Western food rations dwindled—peanut butter, tuna, and chocolate, which we had painstakingly carried across the border—selfishness.

I wrote in my journal:

> *As God positions my eye over the eyepiece, I pull back, not wanting to see all that festers in my heart. Yet as He drops the iodine of His Spirit upon the slide, these bacteria can no longer hide. My heart is revealed. As a patient Teacher, He leaves me not alone in shame, but gently*

guides me to be transparent about my sins and failures. As I do, He then drops upon the slide the solution I most desperately need—His blood, which covers all my sin.

As Christ's blood sprinkles over our hearts, the bacteria mysteriously disappears. Though our bodies feel soiled with sin, He washes them clean with pure water (Hebrews 10:22). He scoops us up into His arms, restores our broken spirits, dries our tears, and holds us close to His heart.

As I come into the presence of God—the One who has searched me and who knows me, the One who perceives my thoughts from afar, the One who is familiar with all my ways (Psalm 139:1–3)—I can swing open the door of my heart and proclaim, "Come in, Lover of my soul. Search my heart! Know me!" I can emerge from behind the bushes, drop the fig leaves, and be naked before my God. But sometimes taking steps toward this can be scary.

One night as I stepped out of the shower, I heard these words from a song on my CD player:

Tears have flowed
So deep through me.
You have seen
All of me.
Love of my life,
Carry me to Your light;
Every breath that I breathe,
All of me.[2]

The Spirit stirred within me the urge to lay prostrate, humbling myself before the Lord in worship. Though I felt a bit awkward lying physically bare, I resisted my inclination to grab a towel and remained there with my face on the carpet. I cried out to Him—allowing my nakedness to symbolize my willingness to lay my life bare before Him. No fig leaves to cover me. Utterly known by Him who sees all. Utterly dependent upon Him who gives me breath.

A. W. Tozer wrote,

> How unutterably sweet is the knowledge that our heavenly Father knows us completely. No talebearer can inform on us, no forgotten skeleton can come tumbling out of some hidden closet to abash us and expose our past; no unsuspected weakness in our characters can come to light to turn God away from us, since He knew us utterly before we knew Him.[3]

As I worshiped God that evening, the more aware I became of His greatness the more I became acutely aware of my nakedness. For as He reveals himself, we ourselves are revealed before Him.

After that experience I journaled:

> *As I lay here spiritually bare before God, without garments of pretense, unadorned by accessories of accomplishments, I realize I have nothing to offer Him, nothing that He needs, nothing that was not first given by Him, but—and herein lies the mystery—everything He wants. All of me. Not just the effective, the pretty, the useful, but the good, the bad, and even the ugly that He may use all of me for His purposes.*

Though I had been tempted to hide my spiritual and physical nakedness, only when I remained before Him did I realize that He is not the One *from* whom we are to hide, but the One *in* whom we are to hide. God himself is our hiding place (Psalm 32:7).

When we truly understand the gospel of grace, we are free to be transparent about our frailties, fears, and longings. No longer relying upon "having it all together," we acknowledge that we don't. No longer do we pretend we're something that we are not—we realize Christ is everything for us. We are free to be real not only before God but also before others.

COMING OUT OF HIDING BEFORE OTHERS

How can I tell her? I asked God, a bit perturbed that once again He was calling me to take the first step of confession. Every night of the past week as Desirée and I prayed together before going to bed, the Spirit convicted me of sinful attitudes or words I needed to confess from the day. As the differences between Desirée and me—the only two foreigners and believers in the city—began rubbing against each other, we could not escape dealing with even small relational tensions. Little jealousies in relationships with Chinese colleagues, simmering resentments over minor annoyances, daily frustrations with different living habits, all began piling up, building walls between us, stumbling blocks to ministering together.

After several nights of vulnerability before her, I protested to the Lord, *That's* it. *Why do I always have to be the one humbling myself and acknowledging my wrongs? Why don't you convict her?*

His Word sliced through my stubborn thoughts: *"God is opposed to the proud, but gives grace to the humble"* (1 Peter 5:5).

As we bowed together, I apprehensively humbled myself and said to her, "I want to confess. . . ."

The next night to my surprise and relief, she initiated: "I also have something to confess. . . ."

"You know, Stacey," she later acknowledged, "if you hadn't been so open and honest, I would have never shared what I did. When you are honest with me, it makes me want to be honest, too, and helps me become more comfortable acknowledging when I have been wrong."

Relieved, I wrote in my journal:

> *Oh, what a glorious time this is to live with one person from whom I cannot hide, with whom we only have two*

*options—to be prideful or to be humble. . . . Though Satan
tempts us to hide our sins in fear of rejection, being honest
before others leads to deeper intimacy and love.*

Ten years later, the challenge to be real—to be humble about
my failures, transparent about my sin—continues. As I talked
with Desirée (who now lives two thousand miles away) on the
phone last week, I confessed how I'd recently fallen short of
obedience in an area in my life. Though she would not have
known about it, I wanted her to hold me accountable to be faithful to what God had directed me to do.

Still, as I revealed to her my disobedience to God, I risked
losing her respect. During that phone call, I again experienced
(as I had ten years earlier) the mystery of honesty: When we are
transparent about ourselves, rather than driving others and God
away, more often than not our honesty actually draws them
closer.

The next day Desirée responded in an e-mail: "I just wanted
to say thanks for being so honest and humble. I know it's not
easy to deal with that kind of stuff, but . . . I always respect you
even more after such confessions." Somehow, honesty—though
it seemingly will cause others to think less of us—often increases
intimacy and even respect. God, in His grace, exalts us as we
humble ourselves before Him (James 4:10). Desirée's response
was nothing short of God's grace in calling me out of hiding and
encouraging me to come before Him and others as I am.

COMING OUT OF HIDING BEFORE OURSELVES

Why is it so hard to be honest about who we really are? We
strive to be what we *think* God wants us to be, often squeezing
ourselves into a cookie-cutter image of what we envision as a
"strong Christian." We attempt to model someone we might consider spiritual, when, in some cases, their charisma and dyna-
mism may be due more to personality than anything. We all

need role models to inspire us. Yet when we cloak ourselves with what we assume we "should" be, we conceal who we really are. In order to be true to ourselves—the unique creation God has made—and true to God, who has created us for His glory, we must know ourselves.

Martin Buber, in his book *The Way of Man*, relays a traditional Hasidic story of a young man who asks his rabbi how he could ever serve in ways as meaningful as his Jewish forefathers. The rabbi responds: "It is the duty of every person in Israel to know and consider that he is unique in the world in his particular character and that there has never been anyone like him. . . ." He encourages the young man to develop his unique potential rather than seek to replicate what another has achieved.

In leaving, he reminds the young man of a wise comment of another rabbi named Zusya, who said shortly before his death: "In the world to come, I shall not be asked: 'Why were you not Moses?' I shall be asked, 'Why were you not *Zusya*?' "[4]

In my pursuit to become more "spiritual" in my early days as a believer, I often neglected the very real human that God had created me to be. My picture of how a super-spiritual woman appeared did not allow for the uniqueness of my personality. Therefore, I assumed my uniqueness was unimportant. Often hesitant to be real about who I was (and was not, though I very much wanted to be), I too easily reached for clothing worn by those I considered more godly. I did not realize that growing in spirituality also involves growing in humanity. As God continues to sanctify our humanness, we become more our true selves. And mysteriously, the more we become our true selves, the more clearly we reveal Christ.

On a recent birthday, I opened a carefully wrapped gift box from my mother containing a brightly painted plaque, stating: *"Angels fly so high because they take themselves lightly."* When we're honest about who we are—and are not—we become free to let go of our uptightness. We're free to be directed by the Spirit within us rather than the approval of those around us. We experience liberation in our lives, for "where the Spirit of the Lord is, there is liberty" (2 Corinthians 3:17).

Each of us has been created for God's glory (Isaiah 43:7). He calls us honored and precious in His sight (Isaiah 43:4). When I am fully the woman God designed me to be, I affirm God's proclamation that creation is good, and I honor what He has created. When I water down my unique personality (for example, tempering my excitement for simple things out of fear I might appear childish), belittle my unique gifts, and hide my unique weaknesses—when I am not fully myself—I am not fully alive. Moreover, my rejection of God's one-of-a-kind design in me dishonors Him.

Pretense clouds the mirror we are that reflects the glory of God (2 Corinthians 3:18). Being our authentic selves wipes clear the cloudiness, allowing God to shine most brilliantly through us. As a diamond sparkles with many facets, we each reflect a facet of God. As we trust God's inimitable design in creating us, we can leave behind others' expectations. We are freed to be fully ourselves, fully human, fully alive.

Observing the importance of authenticity, Brennan Manning writes,

> To open yourself to another person, to stop lying about your loneliness and your fears, to be honest with your affections, and to tell others how much they mean to you— this openness is a sign of the dynamic presence of the Holy Spirit. . . . To ignore, repress, or dismiss our feelings is to fail to listen to the stirrings of the Spirit within our emotional life.[5]

Perhaps one of the most challenging forums in which to be ourselves is meeting someone of the opposite gender when we are desiring a relationship. As we seek to know them and be known, we face the most critical time to be authentically ourselves, yet also the greatest temptation to hide our real selves. What if they don't like who we truly are? They might reject us.

As I began dating a man, when he expressed how strongly he felt about me, my first thought was: *But you hardly even know me.* Though we had enjoyed many dates together, I feared that once he *really* got to know me, he would not like me. I came close to ending the relationship to spare myself the pain of potential rejection.

But one night he asked me to share from my journal—a window to my soul. As I did, albeit selectively and with great trepidation, his positive and warm response surprised me. Revealing my deepest self—what I most feared would drive him away—actually drew him closer.

I learned that night that intimacy can only go so deep without the risk of vulnerability. When I'm tempted to hide my true self, I withhold blessing others with whom God has uniquely made me. If I present what I think someone is looking for, I smudge the spectacles of my heart and can't see whether or not the real me is the best match for the real them.

We must settle for nothing less, in ourselves or in others, than being who we really are. God will honor our integrity—either blessing us with a relationship or sparing us from one that is not best—as we truly reveal our selves. "No good thing does He withhold from those who walk uprightly" (Psalm 84:11).

THE GIFT OF BEING OURSELVES

"We give glory to God simply by being ourselves."
—Brennan Manning[6]

During one of the more difficult times in my life, when I felt I had little to offer others, a friend assured me: "You are a blessing just in who you are." When I am most myself, my true self—not someone I think others want or expect me to be, but instead am freely, joyfully, unashamedly Stacey—I glorify God.

Martin Buber noted that "man cannot escape the eye of God, but in trying to hide from Him, he is hiding from himself."[7] As we come out of hiding before God, we discover our true selves. And though our temptation is to hide behind a facade, our true self is the one God wants to use to bless others. As we embrace the mystery of honesty, we increasingly become the unique person God has created.

The father of a friend of mine, before she went out at night, used to send her off with a simple reminder: "Remember who you are." If we listen, we just might hear God say this to us.

THE MYSTERY OF HONESTY: REFLECTIONS

QUESTIONS FOR JOURNAL AND/OR SMALL GROUP

1. Where do you hide from God, others, and yourself? In what area of your life is He calling you to come out of hiding?
2. With whom do you want to be more open and vulnerable? What risk can you take today to become more vulnerable with someone? With God?
3. What are some ways God has uniquely created you?
4. What have others commented they like, appreciate, or simply notice about you?
5. How can you take yourself less seriously?
6. Take some time in prayer to thank God for whom He has created you to be. Agree with Him that His creation is good. Ask Him to help you think the thoughts He does about you.

BE WHAT YOU ARE

Be what you are!
Simple . . .

But the fact is many of us find it difficult
to accept this fundamental.
We keep trying to be what we are not . . .
were never intended to be.
Life is a constant battle against built-in limitations.
Like trying to be a concert artist when one cannot sing.
Instead of accepting ourselves as we are . . .
As God made us to be.
We struggle to be like somebody else.
Somebody with different talents and gifts.
Somebody God intended to be unique.
As He intended each of us to be unique.
Intimidated by the seeming superiority of another,
we ignore our uniqueness.
Meanwhile, we sacrifice what we are.
One will never become what he can be
until he accepts what he is!
You are the only you God gave to the world . . .
Be yourself!
—Dick Halverson, former Chaplain of the U.S. Senate

VERSES TO TREASURE

He knows the secrets of the heart. (Psalm 44:21)

No creature is hidden from His sight, but all things are open and laid bare to the eyes of Him. (Hebrews 4:13)

Thou dost hide them in the secret place of Thy presence. (Psalm 31:20)

They looked to Him and were radiant, and their faces shall never be ashamed. (Psalm 34:5)

I acknowledged my sin to Thee, and my iniquity I did not hide. I said, "I will confess my transgressions to the Lord." . . . *Thou art my hiding place.* (Psalm 32:5, 7)

BEING REAL WITH OTHERS

God, why is it so hard to get so close to people . . .
to let people get close to me . . . to make friends?
Is it because I've been hurt before . . .
and am afraid to be vulnerable again?
Is it because I think others will take advantage
of my openness?
Your Son had twelve close friends . . .
One sold him for thirty pieces of silver . . .
Another denied that he had ever known him . . .
the rest ran away when he needed them most.
Jesus even predicted these things . . .
yet he didn't shut himself off from friendship.
Make me willing to take the risk too . . .
Help me realize that ultimately,
in opening to another human being,
I am opening myself to you. Amen.

—Source unknown

THOUGHTS FOR CONTEMPLATION

"When you know that you are known, you are no longer the same."

—Walter Wangerin, storyteller and author

"Therefore there is only one problem on which all my existence, my peace and my happiness depend: to discover myself in discovering God. If I find Him I will find myself, and if I find my true self I will find Him."

—Thomas Merton, *New Seeds of Contemplation*

"Without knowledge of self, there is no knowledge of God."
—John Calvin, *Institutes of the Christian Religion*

"Do you know what you are? You are a marvel. In all the world there is no one exactly like you."
—Pablo Casals, Spanish cellist, conductor, and composer

GUIDED MEDITATION:
SELECTIONS FROM PSALM 139

O Lord, Thou hast searched me and known me.

Ask the Holy Spirit to come and search you now as you sit in silence before Him.

Thou dost know when I sit down and when I rise up; Thou dost understand my thoughts from afar. Thou dost scrutinize my path and my lying down, and art intimately acquainted with all my ways.

Review the day, and picture Jesus with you through each of its activities: at work, conversing with family, friends, while you exercise, talk on the phone, drive. . . . Relish His closeness to you.

Where can I go from Thy Spirit? Or where can I flee from Thy presence?

How might you be hiding from God? How are you fleeing from Him?

If I ascend to heaven, Thou art there; if I make my bed in Sheol, behold, Thou art there. If I take the wings of the dawn, if I dwell in the remotest part of the sea, even there Thy hand will lead me, And Thy right hand will lay hold of me.

Take time to praise God that His presence is with us wherever we go . . . that He is with us even when we hide from Him.

I will give thanks to Thee, for I am fearfully and wonderfully made; wonderful are Thy works, and my soul knows it very well.

Take time to meditate upon this truth, repeating and absorbing it deep into your heart: "I am fearfully and wonderfully made by God!"

My frame was not hidden from Thee, when I was made in secret, and skillfully wrought in the depths of the earth.

Thank you, Lord, that even what is secret to others, or to myself, is not secret to you. I can be fully honest with you about the secret things in my heart because you already know them all. Nothing I will share with you or tell you can ever take you by surprise. This truth brings me great consolation.

How precious are Thy thoughts to me, O God! How vast is the sum of them! If I should count them, they would outnumber the sand.

Take time to go to a beach where you can feel the countless grains of sand, or to sit under the millions of stars and consider how God's thoughts toward us are more numerous than all the grains or stars.

Search me, O God, and know my heart; Try me and know my anxious thoughts; and see if there be any hurtful way in me, and lead me in the everlasting way.

Take time to be still and allow God to search your heart. Rest in His care to lead you in the right way.

HYMN: "Rock of Ages"

Rock of Ages, cleft for me,
Let me hide myself in Thee;
Let the water and the blood,
From Thy wounded side which flowed,
Be of sin the double cure;
Save from its guilt and power.

Not the labors of my hands
Can fulfill Thy law's demands.
Could my zeal no respite know,
Could my tears forever flow,
All for sin could not atone;
Thou must save, and Thou alone.

Nothing in my hand I bring,
Simply to Thy cross I cling;
Naked, come to Thee for dress,

Helpless, look to Thee for grace.
Foul, I to the fountain fly;
Wash me, Savior, or I die.

While I draw this fleeting breath,
When mine eyes shall close in death,
When I soar to realms unknown,
See Thee on Thy judgment throne,
Rock of Ages, cleft for me;
Let me hide myself in Thee.

FURTHER READINGS

"The important thing is to stop lying to yourself. A man who lies to himself, and believes his own lies, becomes unable to recognize truth, either in himself or in anyone else, and he ends up losing respect for himself as well as for others. When he has no respect for anyone, he can no longer love and, in order to divert himself, having no love in him, he yields to his impulses, indulges in the lowest forms of pleasure, and behaves in the end like an animal, in satisfying his vices. And it all comes from lying—lying to others and to yourself."

—Fyodor Dostoevsky, *The Brothers Karamazov*

"All of us are sinners. And we are not going to cease being sinners by redoubling our efforts at being good. Living in the open means that we don't have to hide who we really are, whitewash our reputations or disguise our hearts. We can be open about who we are, about what we have thought and felt and done. We don't have to exhaust ourselves to project the blame for who we are on God or on our parents or on society. We don't have to make up fancy excuses. How refreshing that is!"

—Eugene Peterson, *Traveling Light*

PRAYER

Father, you have been revealing to me my deep-seated fears about coming closer to you. Lord, sometimes I'm afraid; afraid of revealing my heart before you and others; afraid of rejection. I fear what I will see in myself when illumined by the vibrant light of your holiness.

Yet I thank you that seeing all, knowing all, and perceiving all, you still choose me in Christ. When like Adam I am tempted to hide my nakedness from you, you call me to run into your arms and hide myself in you.

Help me, Lord, to be real before you, real before others, and real even before myself. Help me to be more human, knowing that Jesus came to redeem us not from our humanness, but from our sin.

Thank you, God, that as you want me to reveal more of myself to you, you are longing to reveal more of yourself to me.

2
BEAUTY AND THORNS:

THE MYSTERY OF LOVE

To love at all is to be vulnerable. Love anything, and your heart will certainly be wrung and possibly broken. If you want to make sure of keeping it intact, you must give your heart to no one, not even to an animal. Wrap it carefully round with hobbies and little luxuries; avoid all entanglements; lock it up safe in the casket or coffin of your selfishness. But in that casket—safe, dark, motionless, airless—it will change. It will not be broken; it will become unbreakable, impenetrable, irredeemable. The alternative to tragedy, or at least the risk of tragedy, is damnation. The only place outside Heaven you can be perfectly safe from all dangers and perturbations of love is Hell.

C. S. Lewis, *The Four Loves*

Love bears all things.

1 Corinthians 13:7

"GOOD NIGHT," I said, turning to go inside. Suddenly he grabbed my hand from behind, pulling me close. As he slipped his arms around my waist, a shot of adrenaline—fear and excitement—rushed through every cell in my body. We stood silently in the warmth of the early September evening, my back against his chest. Too frozen to turn and look at him, I fixed my eyes on the full moon shining against the dark autumn sky.

We had met six weeks earlier at a murder-mystery party. Throughout the game, with each participant playing a potentially guilty character, we questioned each other for clues. After the game, John and I continued to playfully pry each other for information—this time about our personal lives. One week later, the phone rang at my office. With shakiness in his voice, he asked me to lunch.

Though I'd assumed we had little in common, the ease and laughter I enjoyed with John during our date surprised me. This man, quite different from the type with whom I imagined myself, soon began to intrigue me. He disarmed me with his transparency, tickled me with his humor, captivated me with his depth. Walk after walk and talk after talk, he wove his way deeper and deeper into the fabric of my heart. That night under the stars, I stood on the brink of falling in love.

But love frightened me—especially the unknowns. It was all such a mystery. *Should I open my heart without a guarantee that I won't be hurt? What if I begin to love him more than he loves me? Will he love me when he sees the parts I don't like about myself?*

Doubt chimed in: *He and I are much too different. Besides, I just accepted a scholarship for graduate school in England, and I'll be leaving next fall. After that, I want to return to work in China long-term. Won't getting involved with him only set both of us up for future pain?*

But should I close myself off to love unless it (and he) clearly fits in my little box of what love should look like? Even with these questions, for the first time in my life, my heart was becoming deeply intertwined with a man's.

Is this what love is—finding your lists turned inside out and your world turned upside down? Is this what love requires—risk when there is no certainty a relationship will work? To step forward when so many questions remain unanswered, yet strangely feeling drawn to find out where this mysterious path will lead? Though I had no answers, something beckoned me forward.

"Sometimes there is just no rational explanation for why and when we feel linked to another," write husband and wife authors Frederic and Mary Ann Brussat. "*Mystery* is at the heart of intimate relationships."[1]

In my relationship with John, I found myself right in the middle of this mystery.

Mystery *does* lie at the heart of intimate relationships, *all* intimate relationships—with friends, family, soul mates. Especially mysterious is the relationship between a man and a woman. The wise King Solomon wrote, "There are three things which are too wonderful to me, four which I do not understand: The way of an eagle in the sky, the way of a serpent on a rock, the way of a ship in the middle of the sea, and the way of a man with a maid" (Proverbs 30:18–19). As we embrace this mystery, we experience the incredible power and paradoxes of love.

What unimaginable power is this that draws two complete strangers together—who, until meeting, had lived quite happily without each other—in such a way that now they cannot imagine spending their lives apart? What could enable us to expose the depths of our heart to another with no guarantee we won't be hurt? What paradox is this that the one who delights you more than any other can also frustrate you more than any other? That the one whose words have power to lift you to the heights can also cut you to the depths? That the one who can bring you tears of joy can also cause you tears of pain? That two distinct individuals can cleave together and become one in marriage? As the apostle Paul says, *"This mystery is great"* (Ephesians 5:32, italics added).

When we consent to love, we give the one we love indescribable power over us. And, holding their heart, we wield power over them—power to heal or to hurt, to build up or to tear down, to beautify or to belittle. Love has the strength to bring out the best and the worst in us and in our beloved. We are given a choice as to how we will use the power of love.

"Of all powers," writes Frederick Buechner, "love is the most powerful and the most powerless. It is the most powerful because it alone can conquer that final and most impregnable stronghold that is the human heart. It is the most powerless because it can do nothing except by consent."[2]

Only by consenting to love, with its many paradoxes, do we experience its power to transform our lives.

TRUE LOVE

What is true love? Romantic movies portray love as overpowering feelings of attraction inspiring two people to naturally care for and serve each other.

Yet the love that Jesus calls us to describes a volitional rather than purely emotional choice. Strong feelings of attraction usually do precipitate a love relationship—like revving up a car before shifting it into gear. But for the car to move forward, it must run on fuel. For a relationship to move beyond merely revved up emotions, *choice* and *action* must fuel it. True love chooses to serve, even when feelings of love waver—or worse, when feelings of frustration and hate surface.

The biblical word *agape*, describing how to love those dear to us, is the identical word used in describing how to love our enemies. Why would God use the same word? I think He knew that some days, even our dearest loved one can feel like our enemy. As much as we'd like to believe we'll naturally love our spouse, siblings, or friends, there are days we won't. Jesus knew how difficult it is to act loving even when we don't feel like it, and how tempted we are to confuse true love with strong emotions. Consequently, He made it simple for us: *"Therefore, however you want people to treat you, so treat them"* (Matthew 7:12).

True love is not merely *getting* what we want but *giving* what we want. It's about meeting others' needs, not waiting to see who best meets ours.

After a period in any dating and marriage relationship, feelings will lose their intensity and issues may develop. *But where did the glory and excitement go? we wonder. What happened to the thrill and certainty that this relationship was ideal?*

When I worked in Indiana, I relished the beauty of spring after the long, icy winter. One day as I walked out of my office, my breath stopped when I the saw the pear trees lining the walkway. Donning thousands of blossoms, they appeared adorned in dazzling white wedding dresses. I stood for several minutes, taking in the glorious display. However, a few weeks later, the petals that entranced me had fallen to the ground and blown away.

Love may feel a bit like that. Yet feelings, like petals, are only the precursor to the choice fruit of the tree. When the blossoms fall, the pear—and the real fruit of love that feeds our lives—can begin to grow.

C. S. Lewis observed,

> Being in love is a good thing, but it is not the best thing. There are many things below it, but there are also things above it. You cannot make it the basis of a whole life. It is a noble feeling, but it is still a feeling. Now, no feeling can be relied on to last in its full intensity, or even

to last at all. Knowledge can last, principles can last, habits can last; but feelings come and go. And, in fact, whatever people say, the state called "being in love" usually does not last.

But of course ceasing to be "in love" need not mean ceasing to love. Love in this second sense—love as distinct from "being in love" is not merely a feeling. It is a deep unity, maintained by the will and deliberately strengthened by habit; reinforced by . . . the grace which both ask, and receive, from God. They can have love for each other even when they do not like each other; as you love yourself even when you do not like yourself.[3]

When we willfully choose to love even at moments when the other—be it our spouse, friend, co-worker, or enemy— seems hardest to love, we experience one of the mysterious paradoxes of life. Our very acts of love, when we don't particularly feel like loving, ignites feelings of affection.

Reverend Tim Keller described this phenomenon from his experience of months of counseling, helping, and ministering to a very difficult couple, the "Smiths." On his day off, his wife asked what he wanted to do, and he responded, "Why don't we ask the Smiths to get together with us?"

"Why would you want to spend time with *them* on your day off?" his wife asked incredulously.

The Smiths were not the type of couple with whom most people wanted to spend any time. It then dawned on him that in counseling and helping them—in treating them with love— he had actually grown to like them and enjoy spending time with them!

THE POWER OF CHOICE

In romantic relationships, we may assume, "I will always feel love for my beloved." In reality, there are days we won't. But when the petals of feelings fall around our feet, we can still choose to practice love. We nurture the fruit of true love by treating others with honor even when the feelings have blown away.

Three months after my moonlit night with John, I walked into my office to find a stunning bouquet of purple irises with three red roses on my desk. The note attached to the flowers read, "For our three moons together. In hope of many more." In those early months, John was the easiest person in the world to love. But as the petals fell—such as during our first major argument—I learned about loving when I didn't feel like it.

"I am going to get really angry if we keep talking about this," he snapped as he pulled the car in front of my apartment building.

"So we have to stop because *you* want to?" I retorted. "*I think we need to resolve this now.*"

After a curt response from him, I got out of the car and slammed the door behind me. As I ran toward my apartment door, a verse stopped me dead in my tracks: *"Do not let the sun go down on your anger"* (Ephesians 4:26).

My pride screamed, *Don't listen to Him! What does He know?! Go straight ahead and don't look back!*

But my heart, pierced by God's Word, made me turn around and walk back to John's car, where he stood. "I'm sorry for getting angry."

Stone-faced, he pulled back from me as I reached out to hug him.

"Why did you come back?" he asked coldly.

"Because I don't want us to let the sun go down on our anger. Let's just forgive each other for now and deal with it tomorrow."

"The sun already went down," he shot back with the jolt of a sawed-off shotgun.

My heart froze. I had wounded him more deeply than I realized. Yet I, too, hurt from the sting of his words during our argument. His cold response to my attempts at reconciliation burned like frostbite upon my heart.

I ran inside. My sobs awoke my roommate, who came and stroked my back, comforting me while tears poured down my face. *How could he have said the things he did? How could I have hurt him so badly? I love him, Lord, so why are we fighting like this?*

I awoke early the next morning and prayed. As I read the Ephesians passage that had turned my feet around the night before, this time another verse struck me: "Be kind to one another, tender-hearted, forgiving each other, just as God in Christ also has forgiven you" (4:32).

Selfishness told me to wait to forgive him until *he* made the first step; after all, I'd already tried once. Yet as I meditated on how Christ forgave me—fully and completely, when I did not deserve it—I knew I had to humble myself and ask John's forgiveness whether or not I thought he also should ask for mine.

Only by the help of God's Spirit and Word could I drive to his house and apologize before he left for work. Only by God's Spirit could I love the way Christ calls us to love. And only by God's help can we see and dwell on the good even when we have been hurt.

Some time later while strolling through a museum I passed a display case. Precious jewels and stones sparkled behind glass. A royal-purple amethyst caught my attention, and I marveled at its beauty. But thoughts of John's abrasive words from previous arguments scraped against my heart, distracting me from the beauty of the jewels. As I dwelt on what bothered me, I wondered, *How can I love him as Jesus calls me to?*

Rounding a corner in the museum, I nearly walked into a huge purple amethyst stone on display. It was the first time I had seen a cross-section of the entire rock. Though the jewel dazzled at its core, the exterior looked rough, jagged, dark gray—and very unattractive. Had I stumbled upon this rock in nature, I would have judged it worthless.

However, beneath that rough and unappealing exterior, the precious amethyst sparkled. By focusing on John's abrasiveness, I was carelessly overlooking the beauty within him—the delightful gems in his heart.

I remembered that the apostle Paul exhorted the Philippian believers,

> *Whatever is true, whatever is honorable, whatever is right, whatever is pure, whatever is lovely, whatever is of good repute, if there is any excellence and if anything worthy of praise let your mind dwell on these things.* (4:8)

By dwelling upon the many praiseworthy qualities that I treasured in John, my attitude toward him softened.

PARADOX OF PAIN AND LOVE

As John and I continued to grow close, I began to learn another paradox of love. The deeper we opened ourselves to intimacy, the greater became our vulnerability to hurt. Before "falling in love," I assumed that true love would never sting. Bewildered, I asked God, *Lord, if this is truly love, why do we experience such wounding? Why does love at times deeply hurt if it is supposed to be so good?*

As I cried out to Him, I sensed His response in my spirit:

"Stacey, I am with you. I see your hurt. . . . I know your pain. . . . I, too, suffer much over those I love. I am also hurt by those I love. And yet, who said that love does not involve pain? There is much to learn in it. Never let anguish hold you back from loving someone, lest this world shrivel up in death."

But God, isn't there someone else who wouldn't cause me pain?

"Not if you really love. For love on this side of the cross involves hurt. . . . Yet I continued to walk toward that cross,

bearing in mind the joy set before me—the joy of having you in glory with me forever."

The paradox of pain coexisting with love struck me again when I visited the Coventry Cathedral in England. Decimated by German bombs during an eleven-hour raid in World War II, only a blackened shell of the original structure remained. But next to it stood the new massive cathedral. Erected by funds from German and British churches, it served as a tribute to forgiveness and reconciliation.

As I strolled through the inside, I meditated on Jesus' words chiseled on twenty-foot-high bronze tablets. One particularly struck me: *"A new commandment I give unto you that ye love one another as I have loved you."* How did He love us? In the bottom corners of the tablets, two engraved hands each bore a hole in the middle.

Though He faced great agony on the cross, Jesus did not hold back his love. Rather, He "demonstrates His own love toward us, in that while we were yet sinners, Christ died for us" (Romans 5:8). He walked toward the cross, directly into the depths of anguish, to demonstrate the depths of His love.

I read an interesting comment in a book on relationships by Walter Trobisch: "It pays to suffer lover's grief." Though love involves pain, and sometimes sorrow, pain is not pointless. As we open ourselves to the possibility of being deeply wounded, we also open ourselves to the possibility of deeper love. The closer we get to the fragrance of the rose, the greater chance its thorns can prick us, but the richer the scent we enjoy.

In her book *Magnificant*, Ruth Obbard asserts,

> True love is suffering love. Why? Because we are naturally selfish, and to come close to another we have to break through painful barriers. If we go out to another, give ourselves in any way to another, we make "the other" important, we expose ourselves to hurt, and this is painful for our ego.[4]

Not only do we experience pain in love, but we find ourselves at times hurting those we love the most. Our selfishness deters us from serving others. One of my newlywed friends observed,

> I've thought, *I've never been selfish or prideful. What are you talking about?* In reality, my sin has always been there, and I've been running from it or hiding it when it surfaced. But when you are with someone day and night, you can't run or hide. . . . Josh loves me first, then allows me to see my sin. His love, tenderness, and patience allow me to change. Thank God.

"Relationships," write Frederic and Mary Ann Brussat, "provide us with opportunities to practice enthusiasm, gratitude, hospitality, love, play. . . . At the same time, they may expose our shadow sides, drawing out our anger, envy, hatred, pain, greed, and shame. These bonds also constantly school us in the spiritual practice of mystery."[5]

THE POWER OF LOVE

In this practice of mystery, as we choose to love even when we see each other's shadow sides, we experience love's beautifying power. Another friend of mine who recently married wrote me, saying,

> These months have gone by so fast, and we are more deeply in love. I respect him even more than when we were dating, when I hadn't yet seen some of his imperfections that you see only in marriage! I also continue to realize how dependent we are on God to keep the relationship healthy and growing: When one of us is out of sync with God, it affects the relationship. No longer can I hide my sin!

Love enables us not to deny the imperfections in another, but to accept and even embrace the person in the face of his short-comings. And as we depend upon God, He shapes us, and our beloved, to become more like Christ.

One afternoon while walking alone, I began thinking and praying about my relationship with John. I thought about the parts of him that I hoped might change.

As I walked across a freshly cut green soccer field, I looked down and saw a smooth brown stone that fit perfectly in my hand. *How strange,* I thought. *This is a stone from the seashore, worn perfectly smooth by thousands of years of water washing over it. But here it lies in the middle of a field, hundreds of miles from an ocean!* I reached to pick it up, and the moment my hand touched its smooth surface, I sensed God say, *"I smooth the stone."*

Through this, God showed me: *"It's not your work to change John and smooth his rough edges. It's mine."*

Three weeks later, as I purchased an item at a gift shop, a box of colorful polished stones caught my eye. I picked up an amethyst and ran my thumb over its silkiness.

Marveling at its shine and beauty and recalling the words I had sensed God speak to me in the field, a new thought struck me: *"I smooth the stone . . . and* you *polish it."* God had smoothed these stones through nature. Man had polished them to a beautiful shine. It was if He was saying, *"Polish the stone in your hand* [be it John, a family member, a friend] *by your encouragement, praise, gentleness, love . . . and you can make it shine."*

God's love has power to transform our lives and make us beautiful. Our love has power to bring out the beauty in others, to make them shine. Frederick Buechner notes,

> In *Beauty and the Beast*, it is only when the Beast discovers that Beauty really loves him in all his ugliness that he himself becomes beautiful. In the experience of St.

John, it is only when a person discovers that God really loves him in all his unloveliness that he himself starts to become godlike.[6]

Love transforms the beloved. Jesus loved us not because we were lovely; He loved us to make us lovely. He reached out and embraced us—even in all our ugliness—to bring us near to God.

Human love, as passionate and powerful as it can be, merely hints at the passion and power of God's love for us. In romantic love, we fear that when our beloved *really* sees us—when our makeup is off for the night, when we haven't showered, when we have PMS, when we're in a grumpy mood, when we're out of shape—he might no longer love us. We wonder, *Will he still love me when he looks into my closet—of both my home and my heart?*

Yet God's love sees all and loves us still. His love does not sway with emotion, with how nice or unkempt we look, how sweet we are (or aren't). God's love beautifies us even when we feel ugly. God's love completes us even when we feel incomplete. His love gives even when we offer nothing in return. God's love is here to stay.

LOVING GOD'S WAY

After John and I had been dating nearly a year, I began preparing for my graduate scholarship program in England. Around that time, John unexpectedly accepted a two-year teaching position in Africa. On the morning of his departure, we held hands as we sat quietly together in the waiting area, not wanting to talk for fear we could not hold back a deluge of tears.

"Flight 254 to Kenya now boarding," announced the gate attendant. We hugged good-bye, and John joined the line of other international travelers. Just before reaching the gate, he turned, walked back toward me, kissed me, and said, "I love you."

Neither of us knew what would happen in our relationship after living on different continents for two years. Though I did not know if John and I would eventually marry, I reflected in my journal one day:

> *The true mystery of love is not finding someone who is "perfect for me," but instead is laying myself aside to love and serve another, seeking another's good and growth, giving what I want to receive, and loving even beyond the pain. Oh, how far more difficult is that than "finding the right spouse."*

Though at that time the future of our relationship was still a mystery—as were many things about love—I knew that loving, as a friend once told me, is always better than not loving.

And the loving to which I am called each day includes much more than the love of one man, no matter how precious that may be. As we venture into the mystery of love, we are faced with two questions we must always seek to answer: "Am I loving as God calls me to love?" and "Am I using the power of love for good in others' lives?" May our answer always be yes!

THE MYSTERY OF LOVE: REFLECTIONS

QUESTIONS FOR JOURNAL AND/OR SMALL GROUP

1. How can you love someone today as Jesus has loved you?
2. Even if you don't feel like it, how can you choose to love your spouse, friend, family member, or co-worker today?
3. Make a list of your loved one's beautiful qualities. Reflect upon each one for a few minutes. Thank God for those qualities and for how they have blessed your life.
4. How can you "polish" a loved one to help him or her shine?

VERSES TO TREASURE

"You shall love the Lord your God with all your heart, and with all your soul, and with all your mind." This is the great and foremost commandment. And the second is like it, "You shall love your neighbor as yourself." On these two commandments depend the whole Law. (Matthew 22:37–40)

There is no fear in love, but perfect love casts out all fear. (1 John 4:18)

For your Maker is your husband—the Lord Almighty is His Name. (Isaiah 54:5)

And don't be wishing you were someplace else or with someone else. Where you are right now is God's place for you. Live and obey and love and believe right there. God, not your marital status, defines your life. (1 Corinthians 7:17 THE MESSAGE)

Do not awaken love before its time. (Song of Solomon 3:5, author's paraphrase)

THOUGHTS FOR CONTEMPLATION

On God's love:

"We please Him most not by frantically trying to make ourselves good but by throwing ourselves into His arms with all our imperfections, and believing that He understands everything and loves us still."

—A. W. Tozer, *The Knowledge of the Holy*

On loving others:

"Through union with Him (as Augustine said, He is more intimate with us than we are with ourselves), nothing is wasted, nothing is missing. There is never a moment that does not carry eternal significance—no action that is sterile, no love that lacks fruition, and no prayer that is unheard."

—Brennan Manning, *Abba's Child*

"To love another person is to see the face of God."
— Victor Hugo, *Les Misérables*

On marital love:

"Any situation that calls me to confront my selfishness has enormous spiritual value, and I slowly began to understand that the real purpose of marriage may not be happiness as much as it is holiness."
— Gary Thomas, *Sacred Marriage*

"In conventional novels a couple falls deeply in love and then marriage follows as a mere consequence, bringing the story to an end. In actual life it is the other way; often the *deepest love* comes after marriage rather than before and is clearly its consequence."
— Elton Trueblood, *The Common Ventures of Life: Marriage, Birth, Work, Death*

"Each person who marries opens himself voluntarily to pain because he puts himself in a position in which he can more easily be hurt. Every avowed lover is terribly vulnerable, and marriage only accentuates the vulnerability as it accentuates the possible glory."
— Elton Trueblood

On life:

"What is life if you don't have love?"
— Elden Conklin (my grandfather), on his deathbed

WHAT TO FIGHT FOR

If you're going to fight . . .
Fight for the relationship, not against it.
Fight for reconciliation, not alienation.
Fight to preserve friendship, not destroy it.
Fight to save your marriage, not to cash it in.
Fight to solve the problem, not to salve your ego.

If you're going to fight, fight to win, not to lose.
Lasting friendships are not negotiated—they are forged.
That means heat and pressure.
Authentic intimacy comes only through struggle.
Relationships are sustained by commitment, not pleasant
    feelings.
Treat a relationship as negotiable, and it's easily lost.
Consider it non-negotiable, and a way is found to make it
    work.
>   —Dick Halverson, former Chaplain of the U.S. Senate

*Love is patient, love is kind, and is not jealous; love does
not brag and is not arrogant, does not act unbecomingly;
it does not seek its own, is not provoked, does not take into
account a wrong suffered, does not rejoice in unrighteous-
ness, but rejoices with the truth; bears all things, believes
all things, hopes all things, endures all things. Love never
fails.*
>   —1 Corinthians 13:4–8

HYMN: "Love Divine, All Loves Excelling"

Love Divine, all loves excelling,
Joy of heaven, to earth come down;
Fix in us Thy humble dwelling;
All Thy faithful mercies crown.
Jesus, Thou art all compassion,
Pure, unbounded love Thou art;
Visit us with Thy salvation,
Enter every trembling heart.

Breathe, O breathe Thy loving Spirit
Into every troubled breast!
Let us all in Thee inherit,
Let us find that second rest.
Take away our bent to sinning;
Alpha and Omega be;
End of faith, as its beginning,

Set our hearts at liberty.

Finish, then, Thy new creation;
Pure and spotless let us be;
Let us see Thy great salvation
Perfectly restored in Thee:
Changed from glory into glory,
Till in heaven we take our place,
Till we cast our crowns before Thee,
Lost in wonder, love, and praise.

PRAYER

Lord, thank you for those people you have brought into my life whom I love and who love me. Thank you for the mysteries of love that we do not fully understand but that call us to love even in the face of questions and sometimes pain.

Help me to recognize the incredible power of intimacy—to hurt and to heal, to build up and to tear down, to belittle and to beautify. May I always use that power to help my loved ones know how much you love them. When I fail, help me to humble myself before them, and you, asking forgiveness and relying upon your Spirit to help me. And when they fail, help me to forgive them quickly and thoroughly, as Jesus does.

Open my eyes to the beauty within them. May my actions and words seek not to grind away their imperfections but to make their beauty shine.

3

WHEN THE HEART IS PIERCED:

THE MYSTERY OF BROKENNESS

God whispers to us in our pleasures,
speaks to us in our conscience,
but shouts to us in our pains.

C. S. Lewis

A broken and contrite heart, O God, Thou wilt not despise.

Psalm 51:17

"TO OUR FUTURE," he said as we clicked our plastic pic-
nic cups together.

After John returned from Africa, we reconnected initially as
friends. When several months had passed, we again began discussing marriage. As we walked back to his car after an in-depth
talk, he mentioned how relieved he felt in having made a decision to move forward. He poured juice into our glasses and
reached over to interlink my arm with his as we toasted.

Ten days later, he told me we should break up.

John's love, like an arrow, had deeply penetrated my heart.
Though I, too, had reservations about our relationship, I cringed
at the thought of the arrow being pulled out, taking with it bits
of flesh and blood I could never replace.

*Can't you just break the arrow and leave the head intact
inside of me?* I prayed. *Yet, do what you need to, Lord. Pain me
as you must to break me free from that which does not belong
in my heart. Place your fingers in the spot to stop the blood, to
touch and heal the gaping wound, to assure me that I am not
alone.*

In the weeks after our parting, longing and aching for John
followed me like a persistent shadow I could not outrun. As
months passed, anger began hounding my footsteps. Anger
toward John. *Maybe if I hate him, I could get over him more
easily.* Anger toward myself. *Why didn't I end the relationship
earlier when I had so many questions?* Anger toward God. *Why,
when I prayed for guidance, did God let me get involved if He
knew it was only going to cause me pain?* But deep inside I
knew that anger, rather than curing the pain, would only inten-
sify it.

Brokenness. If we open our souls, we will all face it at some
point in our lives. Perhaps it's a broken heart—losing a loved

one through death, divorce, breakup—or a broken dream, a broken childhood, a broken spirit, a broken body, or broken expectations. Maybe it's sharing in the brokenness of another, or simply experiencing the brokenness of being human.

Brokenness hurts. When healing seems to take too long, how tempted we are to reach for painkillers—denial, a new relationship, social activity, busyness—to deaden our agony. Yet Jesus is not interested in numbing our pain but in bringing wholeness. He is not the Great Pharmacist, but the Great Physician.

How do we begin to experience Christ's regeneration? "The first step toward healing," wrote Henri Nouwen, "is not a step away from the pain, but a step toward it."[1] Embracing the pain opens us up to healing—even in places we didn't realize were broken.

I remember as a child breaking my elbow. Frightened and squirming in anguish, I just wanted relief from my pain. Yet the doctor intensified it by insisting I bend my elbow, place its broken tip on a metal table, and move it into different positions while he took X rays. How I wanted to run out of that dark room with all its cold steel equipment and merciless nurses who pinned me to my seat as I cried.

However, the scans showed what none of us had realized—I had broken all three bones in my elbow and needed surgery. Though taking X rays increased my pain, they revealed all that needed healing.

After John and I parted ways, I spoke with the woman who had given us premarital counseling. As I expressed my grief, she commented, "We fear fully embracing our pain because we think God can't handle it, and we have to protect Him." She exhorted me to allow myself time in Gethsemane with Jesus while I was in anguish.

"But what about Paul's words to the Philippians to rejoice always?" I asked.

"You will come to that," she replied. "For now, stay in Geth-semane."

Lord, help me not to fear entering into sorrow and the un-known, I prayed. *Help me to trust that you are greater than the pain. I don't need to pretend it's not there.*

THE TOUCH OF THE HEALER

In embracing pain *as* the first step toward healing, we must also allow Jesus to enter into our woundedness if we want to be restored—and that requires letting go of our grip. I have always loved the old poem that talks about a child bringing her broken toy to God and asking Him to fix it. After some time, she returns to Him and says, "How can you be so slow?" He responds, "My child, you never did let go."

After my breakup with John, in seeking to embrace my pain I began to hold on too tightly. I feared that forgiving John would somehow invalidate the pain he'd caused me, and that total for-giveness would let him off the hook too easily. Besides, I felt so weary of longing for him and hoping for reconciliation with him that ruminating on the ways he had hurt me helped harden my heart toward him. Yet without realizing it, my unwillingness to forgive him erected a wall around my heart barring Jesus from touching my wound.

One morning as my shoulders tensed and my stomach knot-ted I thought, *How could he say such a thing to me?* But this time I couldn't lash back . . . for I was alone in the room, accom-panied only by memories of words he had spoken a year before. Something had triggered a thought, and now the old tapes and old arguments began playing in my mind.

Recalling his stinging words, I hurled a sharp response at him in my imagination. *Bull's-eye!* I put him in his place with direct verbal hits, scoring repeatedly. (Stacey 10, John 0). I was enjoying the sport—until Jesus began refereeing.

"Forgive us our sins as we forgive others who sin against us."

THE MYSTERY OF BROKENNESS / 63

But he doesn't deserve forgiveness! I protested.

"And neither do you."

The truth silenced my imaginary combat. I dropped my head.

O Lord, I cried, *how could these wounds still ache after all this time? Will I ever be healed?*

I then began to see that my unwillingness to forgive John and even myself was like a foot in the door of our relationship, preventing it from fully closing. C. S. Lewis noted that we can't stop the birds from flying over our heads, but we *can* stop them from building nests in our hair. What a nest I had let my negative thoughts build, complete with a birdbath and sunken patio.

The Bible study guide I was using at the time suggested picturing Jesus at the door of my heart. I did that, but then the author urged me to invite Him into the rooms hidden *behind* the closed door of my heart—those dark places where I continued to nurse my wounds. Warily, I opened the door.

As Jesus entered, He quieted my fears with His presence. Yet as He began walking toward my tender flesh, I quickly covered it with my hands. I was not about to let anyone, not even the Great Physician, begin poking around there. Like a child, I whined about my pain while squirming at the sight of a doctor. I preferred nursing the wound on my own, even if my touching it only caused an infection.

As Jesus stood facing my wound, I knew He wanted to lay His hands upon it—to heal it.

But it will hurt! I cried. Yet I knew it was time—time to pull back my hands, time to expose my pain to Him, time to let Him touch me.

I winced. I cringed. Every muscle in my body tightened as His hands descended closer and closer toward the hurt. Fear tempted me to jump back, to push His hands away.

When I finally got the nerve to look down, I still saw wounds. But something was different. They were no longer mine. They were His. Only when I allowed Him to touch my wounds with His could I begin to experience healing. "By His wounds, we are healed" (Isaiah 53:5 NIV).

And when I am tempted to again focus on my wounds, I look and see only the wounds in Jesus' hands—wounds that cleanse me, wounds that heal me, wounds that forgive me, and wounds that enable me to forgive.

WOUNDS FOR GLORY

Though we are a people who are broken, we have a Savior who was broken on our behalf. Jesus came to bind up the brokenhearted, to comfort all who weep, and to give oil of gladness in place of mourning (Isaiah 61:1–3). As His brokenness and wounds mysteriously heal us, they also bring glory to God. Jesus said to His disciples who doubted His resurrection, "Why are you troubled and why do doubts arise in your hearts? See My hands and My feet, that it is I Myself" (Luke 24:38–39).

Jesus points to His wounds to identify His resurrected body. Rather than *remove* Jesus' wounds, God *transformed* Jesus' wounds for glory. They remained part of his *glorified* body! And like Jesus' wounds, ours can be used to glorify God. Contemplating this, Ruth Obbard writes,

> As the wounds of Christ in heaven are the permanent signs of his love, so our own life's wounds can become our glory, for they force us into his loving arms. If we question ourselves closely, we surely see it is our wounds, our unique experience of life's sorrows, that form us as individuals, able to give God praise.[3]

In the amazing mystery of brokenness, the wounded Healer not only heals us, but redeems our wounds for His glory.

TEARS FOR GLORY

God also uses our tears, like our wounds, for His glory. During my brokenheartedness over John, as I searched the

Scriptures for comfort, I was stunned to find so many references to crying. God is not ashamed of our tears, and neither need we be. He is the One who saves all our tears in a bottle (Psalm 56:8). Jesus did not hide His tears when He wept over Jerusalem, nor when He wept at news of Lazarus' death. Tears were precious to Him, like the costly perfume and tears of the woman who anointed His feet (Luke 7:38).

The psalmist describes tears like seeds—the very seeds of joy:

> *Those who sow in tears shall reap with joyful shouting.*
> *He who goes to and fro weeping, carrying his bag of seed,*
> *shall indeed come again with a shout of joy, bringing his*
> *sheaves with him.* (126:5–6)

Mysteriously, sorrow, rather than preventing joy as we often assume, can nurture joy and deepen its intensity. In fact, from the piercing thorn emerges the fragrant rose.

"The difference between shallow happiness and a deep, sustaining joy," writes Walter Wangerin in *Reliving the Passion*, "is sorrow. When sorrow arrives, happiness dies. It can't stand pain. Joy, on the other hand, rises from sorrow and therefore can withstand all grief." The apostle Paul conveys this mystery when he says we are sorrowful yet always rejoicing (2 Corinthians 6:10). And Jesus, who was "full of sorrows and acquainted with grief," is the One who tells us that as we abide in Him our joy will be made full.

NOT IN VAIN

During church one morning, several months after John and I broke up and he moved to another state, my pastor preached about investing our lives in others. As he preached, my throat thickened with pain as I silently prayed, *I did that, Lord. I did that with John. I exposed my soul, I invested my strengths and my weaknesses, my love and my life into that man—and it was all for nothing.*

Yet as the tears trickled onto the church bulletin in my hand, I sensed God whisper to my anguished spirit,

> What you have given to him, you have given and done unto me. You loved *me* when you loved him. You shared your heart with *me* when you shared it with him. You entrusted yourself to *me* when you trusted him. And whether or not he has treasured those things you've given him, *I* have treasured those things. *I* have responded in love to you.

I knew then that my love, my vulnerability, my efforts, my tears were not in vain, for what I gave to John, I gave to the Lord.

BROKENNESS MADE BEAUTIFUL

God says through His prophet Ezekiel, "I will seek the lost, bring back the scattered, bind up the broken" (34:16). As humans, we *all* come into this world broken. Yet only when we suffer the pain of acute brokenness do we realize we cannot fix ourselves. Only then do we understand that Christ, not painkillers, can heal us. But sometimes He needs to place us on the X-ray table to enable us to see the damage. And that can hurt terribly.

My friend, who thought she was strong and whole, recognized her brokenness while under pressure at an extremely intense job. She struggled daily with feelings of incompetence. In honesty she admitted, "I thought I was whole, but in truth I was merely in control holding the pieces together. I didn't know I was broken until that experience when I couldn't hold it together anymore."

When we experience brokenness, we want God to put our lives back just the way they were. But He doesn't. To face their grief at losing their children in a car accident, the parents of two young daughters sought counseling. They were told, "You can't fix this. God can mend your heart, but you will never be the same."[4]

In the midst of our brokenness, our heart and our life lies like shattered bits of glass around us. Piecing the shards back together seems impossible. We will never be able to restore ourselves to be exactly the way we once were. But we don't need to.

We can place our heart in God's hands—and let Him mysteriously exchange our ashes for a garland of beauty. We can let Him build something beautiful from our brokenness. I once read a story about a colorful stained-glass window in a church that broke into hundreds of pieces when someone hurled a rock through it. An artist in the church took the many broken fragments to see what he could do. The window could not be restored to what it had been, but with the remnants he created beautiful candleholders. Though the glass could no longer let the sun shine colorfully through it during the day, it could hold a burning flame of light for those in the midst of the darkness of night.

Our God is *Yahweh Rophe*: The Lord who heals by turning a bitter experience into something sweet.

HELD IN GOD'S EMBRACE

As we attempt to hold the pieces of our brokenness together, Christ calls us to let go and let Him hold them—and, more importantly, hold *us*. Sometimes, when I was really hurting over my loss of love, the only words I could pray were "Hold me, Jesus. Just hold me." And He did.

As we wait for healing of our wounds and beauty from our ashes, we can reach out to Jesus and offer our broken hearts to Him. For "a broken and contrite heart, O God, Thou wilt not despise" (Psalm 51:17).

When we acknowledge our loss and brokenness and hand it to God, we allow ourselves to be embraced more intimately by the Lover of our soul. He takes our broken heart, embraces us, and whispers, *You're blessed when you feel you've lost what is most dear to you. Only then can you be embraced by the One most dear to you.* (Matthew 5:4 THE MESSAGE)

And one day, no matter how hard we weep now, He will wipe every tear from our eyes. But today, when we are too weary to bear our brokenness, the gentle Shepherd lifts us up like a wounded lamb, places us upon His shoulders, and carries us. "Surely our griefs He himself bore, and our sorrows He carried" (Isaiah 53:4).

THE MYSTERY OF BROKENNESS: REFLECTIONS

QUESTIONS FOR JOURNAL AND/OR SMALL GROUP

1. In what area of your life do you need Jesus' healing touch?
2. As an exercise, to someone who has wounded you in the past, write a letter saying something crucial that you were never able to say to that person face-to-face. Pray for God's wisdom in this exercise.*
3. How might God want to use your tears to water seeds of blessings in your life or the lives of others?
4. Write an imaginary trialog (a three-way conversation) between yourself and someone who has been holy, or unholy, in your life. Include Jesus as the third party. When you have finished writing, ask yourself: What did I learn that was new or surprising from my own or the other person's responses? What did Jesus say that made a difference?*

*From a handout on "Journal Exercises" by Luci Shaw, 1999.

VERSES TO TREASURE

"For I will restore you to health, and I will heal you of your wounds," declares the Lord. (Jeremiah 30:17)

Surely our griefs He Himself bore, and our sorrows He carried. (Isaiah 53:4)

I took them in My arms; but they did not know that I healed them. (Hosea 11:3)

In the wilderness . . . the Lord your God carried you, just as a man carries his son, in all the way which you have walked. (Deuteronomy 1:31)

The righteous cry and the Lord hears, and delivers them out of all their troubles. The Lord is near to the brokenhearted, and saves those who are crushed in spirit. (Psalm 34:17–18)

Blessed be the God of our Lord Jesus Christ, the Father of all mercies and God of all comfort; who comforts us in all our affliction so that we may be able to comfort those who are in any affliction with the comfort with which we ourselves are comforted by God. (2 Corinthians 1:3–4)

THOUGHTS FOR CONTEMPLATION

"God wounds us deeply when He wills to heal."
—Hermann Kohlbrugge, *Pastoralblatter*

"I kept still at home in desert places, solitary, weeping. . . . My heart was broken; and when I could sorrow most I had most peace, for something spake to me from the Lord. . . ."
—Francis Howgill, Quaker writer, 1656

"I'm cracked, cracked, cracked, but the thing about cracks is they let the light in."
—Anne Lamott, *Traveling Mercies*

"The deeper that sorrow carves into your heart, the more joy you can contain."

—Kahlil Gibran, *The Prophet*

"The Christian has his sorrows as well as his joys: but his sorrow is sweeter than joy."

—St. John Chrysostom

FURTHER READING

"My recovery from these emotional wounds [the death of her husband at a young age] was in direct proportion to my ability to stop steeling myself against them and begin accepting the pain inherent in my personal loss. I now know that the healing process for any of life's frustrations, disappointments, and sorrows can begin the moment we stop resisting them. Tightly closed hands are not in a position to receive anything—not even comfort. . . . Somehow the cup [of grief] becomes lighter, a little more bearable, and its contents less bitter each time the cup is voluntarily grasped."

—Catherine Marshall, *To Live Again*

PRAYER

Lord, You have welcomed us;
We come to pray for healing in Your love.
Please, as we wait to meet You here,
All doubts, impediments remove.
Redeem our sorrows;
Let our tears become your healing waters blessed.
And lead us, lost, to quiet streams
Where we shall find ourselves refreshed.
Be present in our past, O Lord,
And in the mem'ry of our days.
When terrors of the night oppress,

Protect us in your strong embrace.
Remind us of your faithfulness,
The promise of your presence, Lord.
And keep us trusting in your grace.
Until we greet you whole, restored.

—Jeannette Lindholm

4

FROM STRIVING TO STILLNESS:

THE MYSTERY OF LIMITATIONS

There must come that moment when the believer confesses that all righteousness belongs to God alone. . . . One must come to that point where he has become so weak and so unstable in his own view of himself that he has no recourse left to him but to trust only in the righteousness of God. He recognizes God's all and his own nothingness; God's omnipotence and his own weakness. He is soon, therefore, established in an abandonment that is rarely, if ever, shaken thereafter."

Mme. Jeanne Guyon,
Justification, Vol. II

My grace is sufficient for you, for power is perfected in weakness.
2 Corinthians 12:9

THE RED DIGITAL NUMBERS on my clock flashed 3:00 A.M. as I threw off my sheets, hot and wet from another bout of feverish sweats. Frost lined the windowpane, yet the cold winter night brought little relief to my steaming body. *How long,* I wondered, *will this ritual continue?*

Since completing graduate studies in England and returning to the United States, I could not shake what seemed to be a persistent case of jet lag. No matter how often I slept, debilitating exhaustion hung over me like a weighty cloak. As weeks passed, simple activities became increasingly exhausting. Walking up one flight of stairs felt like climbing a mountain with ten-pound ankle weights strapped to my legs. Even standing—to iron a shirt, wait in a short grocery line, or sing in church—left my head dizzy, my legs burning, and my body shaky.

Where is my energy and strength? This is not me! I anguished. Having always been energetic and buoyant, I knew something was wrong.

With much rest, my body slowly regained some strength. I eagerly started a new job, hoping to make my life again feel "normal." Yet four or five hours into my workday, I had only enough energy remaining to leave my office, drive home, and fall into bed, often too weak to change my clothes.

I visited numerous doctors who poked and scrutinized me. Though none could determine the cause of my sickness, they unanimously told me to rest.

"Rest?!" I protested, "I *have* been resting, and I'm not getting better!" In truth, I stubbornly resisted it, submitting to the doctors' orders to slow down only when I was too weak to do anything else.

"I certainly would love to be ordered by the doctor to simply rest!" an acquaintance commented. But for me—an active and driven twenty-seven-year-old immersed in a culture that lauds productiveness, busyness, and overscheduled Day-Timers—being required to rest felt like a curse, not a blessing. Tell me to take on a new challenge, but don't tell me to rest. *How,* I wondered, *can God have use for me, how can He even really love me if I am lying here doing nothing useful for Him?*

While my body begged me to relax, my mind chanted its typical mantra: *Push harder! Try harder!* After eight months of struggling to continue working while my body battled fatigue and recurrent viruses, I could no longer keep up. I had to leave my job. Though I began physically resting, mentally I chastised myself for neglecting all I "should" be doing. Regardless of how often I rested, a leech-like virus continued to siphon my energy.

As soon as I get over this thing, I can get on with my life! I determined. Yet God had different plans.

One morning, after eighteen months of seeing various doctors, the phone rang. "The blood test results are positive," explained the practitioner I'd seen a few days earlier. "I want you to see a specialist right away." I cringed at the word *specialist,* and visiting her office only confirmed my fears.

In the waiting room sat a patient breathing heavily with the assistance of a shiny metal oxygen tank propped up beside her. Pamphlets explaining illnesses with names I had never heard—polymyalgia rheumatica, ankylosing spondylitis, Sjogren's syndrome, fibromyalgia—lined the walls. Having had robust health for twenty-six years, entering this office was like entering an underground world I never knew existed. Seldom had I thought about my body apart from how to tone it, strengthen it, and nourish it. Now I entered a world in which illness, not willpower, determined what one's body could and could not do.

"Stacey?" the receptionist's voice called me back to the present. After greeting the doctor, I began responding to her litany of questions: "When did you first start noticing symptoms? Have you experienced joint pain? fevers? night sweats? frequent viral infections? achy muscles? sensitivity to sunlight? bruising? a facial rash?" As she continued, the mysterious symptoms—like pieces of a puzzle—began fitting together, rapidly constructing a picture that terrified me.

O God, I prayed, *just let her tell me that I have one of those special cases in which a temporary virus merely mimics a disease.* I wanted to resist revealing all my symptoms for fear they would confirm her tests. As if experiencing an out-of-body phenomenon, I observed the whole conversation and wanted to scream, *"This is not me! You don't understand—I've always been healthy! I've always been energetic! I eat well and exercise! No. You have the wrong person. Pick someone who has not taken care of their health! Pick someone who is not ambitious! Pick someone who doesn't have adventurous plans and dreams for her future! Pick someone who does not want to serve overseas on the mission field!"* Though I had longed to know what ailed me, I never expected my quest to end here.

After reviewing my symptoms and the blood tests, she spread the results across her wide oak desk. Looking up with sympathetic eyes, she spoke the very words I fought so long to avoid, the words that would forever change my life: "You have an incurable disease."

The "strange virus" I had been fighting for the last year and a half was systemic lupus erythematosus—a life-threatening auto-immune disorder. Though created to protect my body from foreign invaders, my immune system no longer could distinguish my own body from a virus, fueling a civil war within me.

While fiercely attacking my body—including joints, muscles, and skin, and threatening my vital organs—my overactive immune system neglected to fight actual viruses, leaving me unprotected against infections.

With solemnity the specialist warned, "This is going to be very difficult for you to live with. I can tell you are a type-A personality. You will need to make some major lifestyle changes." She continued with concern, "Your busy lifestyle and stress level will extremely aggravate your condition and can jeopardize your life."

Like a hurricane hitting without warning, the diagnosis blasted through all the neatly ordered rooms of my life. The furniture I had so painstakingly arranged—my activities, plans, dreams, ministry, work—now lay broken and scattered about. No longer could I find shelter in the hope that my life would soon be back to normal. As if wresting the roof off my home, lupus tore away my sense of being in control. My life now lay fully exposed to the unpredictability of disease and the starkness of my limitations. The truth stared me in the face: I was finite, human, and utterly dependent.

I clung desperately to a life preserver of faith as the waves of doubt crashed over me: *You are going to waste away. God has no use for you now. You'll be lucky if He still loves you. You have nothing to offer Him anymore. All those great plans you had, you can no longer do.*

"God, save me from despair!" I cried out as I lay in bed, surrounded by soggy Kleenexes.

I finally quieted from sobbing long enough to listen to His still, small voice. *"Yes, this does change many of the plans you had. There are many things you wanted to do that you may not be able to do now because of this disease, but you can still do everything that I want you to do. It in no way changes my will for you."*

OUR REAL SOURCE OF WORTH

Only now can I see that unless He'd stopped me in my tracks, I would have continued running ahead of Him, attempting what I presumed were "great things for God" while He watched from the sidelines.

Continuing months of sickness confined me to home and often bed. No longer able to work, to "do ministry" (as I had narrowly defined it), or to take care of myself, let alone serve others, I felt worthless. I felt helpless. I felt hopeless. Most frightening, I felt naked before God. As He gazed at me with His eyes of love, I had no costumes of spiritual activity to hide behind, nothing whatsoever to attract Him. No longer could I reach into my wardrobe of neatly tailored good works to dress me and make me more presentable to Him. Although I knew "our works are like filthy rags before Him," at least emotionally they provided some covering. Now I had not even rags to conceal my desperately unworthy heart. Ashamed of my nakedness before God and others, I yearned to return to "normal" life—active, busy, and striving after new achievements.

The previously unquestioned values upon which I had built my identity—self-reliance, independence, productivity, and drivenness—began splintering like old wooden idols.

Prior to having lupus, I assumed I could accomplish basically whatever I wanted if I was willing to work hard enough. Now the more effort I exerted, the fiercer the illness raged. Not even my best self pep talks could muster my energy. Lupus brought my self-reliance to its knees, exposing the lie under which I had lived for so long: Though I resolutely claimed to believe that God loved me, I lived as if my works (or lack thereof) could increase or diminish the intensity of His affection. No longer self-sufficient, I had to face the truth: I had been striving to earn His approval by my accomplishments. Yet no matter how hard I strove, whatever I did seemed never quite enough to please Him. Now being human with all its limitations was *all* I could be.

One morning I read in my Bible about Jesus ministering to the crowds surrounding Him: "And when evening had come, they were bringing to him all who were ill. . . . And He healed many who were ill with various diseases."

Tears welled in my eyes as I quietly cried, "O Lord, I know you can heal me."

As I waited, I sensed His gentle voice whisper to my crushed heart, *"I can heal you, Stacey, but I want to heal your broken spirit first. Will you let me work on your spirit and wait for my timing to work on your body?"*

O Lord, I prayed, *I want to say, "Heal my body, then I won't have a broken spirit, for only because my body is broken is my spirit broken." But I sense this probably isn't true.*

"Stacey, my concern is to make you holy, to draw you fully to myself. You are so quick to trust in yourself, your own strength, your own abilities, your independence. I want to break you of those things, to break you from fighting me like my servant Jacob, from fighting my plans in your life, my child."

Then a very unexpected thought struck me: *"This disease is my answer to your prayers—for your life to be for my use. Trust me."* The words of Hosea echoed through my mind: *"Come, let us return to the Lord, for He has torn us, but He will heal us; He has wounded us but He will bandage us"* (6:1).

LIVING BY GRACE

As I looked at my life, I envisioned a garden plot of freshly tilled dark soil. Deep grooves in the exposed soil looked naked, lifeless, useless.

What are you doing, Lord? I wanted to cry to the Gardener of my soul. And then I noticed a pile of uprooted weeds lying at the end of the plot. As much as it hurt me, He was tilling my garden to weed from my life the deeply entrenched roots of striving to earn His love.

After several months had passed, I wrote in my journal one morning: *All right, Lord, I am ready to do anything. Just show me your will.*

I waited to hear His still, small voice. *"Anything? What if my will for you is simply to rest?"*

But that is not "something," Lord, I argued. *I'll do anything you want me to* do.

"Anything but this? Then you are not willing to receive any cup I give you—only that which makes sense to you. Must you understand my will to obey it?"

But Lord, I protested, *to rest seems so passive. I want to do something for you, to be something for you.*

My heart sensed His gentle exhortation: *"You can only do after you learn to be, and you will be only by following my leading. Choose quietness during this time, not busyness. Choose stillness, not ambition. Choose listening as your activity, not doing. Take what I have offered you; receive it without having 'earned' it. Visit with me. Draw near to me. Listen to me longingly, for this time together can be precious. This period can pass like a day."*

Even as I heard God's gentle and loving words, my unbelieving spirit still chafed at the thought of rest. As I lay on the couch one day, feeling utterly helpless, I was certain God was busy harvesting great works in the lives of those without limitations like mine. For if I could not produce anything, why would God waste His time on me? I longed for the days filled with activities and people to whom I could minister. Those days made me feel worthwhile and necessary. Now who had need of me? Just lying here, what could I do besides pray? And why would God have any use for me? Again, I cried to Him, *How can you still love me, Lord? I am useless.*

Just then my mom walked into the living room, where I lay on the couch, and reached out her hand to touch my forehead ever so gently. Like a shower of fresh rain, her words watered my parched heart: "Can I get you anything?" Her tone and face expressed such care and patience. How could she be so patient with me when I was so impatient with myself? How could she continue to care for me and serve me month after month—bring me soup, empty my trash can overflowing with tissues, pick up medication for me, take me to the doctors, change my sheets, buy me special foods, listen to my complaints—and all with such love, when I could do nothing for her in return? The more helpless I became, the more grace and love she extended to me. Yet as I thought of God, I had been assuming the more helpless I became, the less He cared or had use for me.

If my mother, who is only human, has even greater compassion on me when I am helpless, how much more is God's love compassionate toward me? It was as if God replied to me through my mother's love: *"That's the point. That's the point, my precious child. And finally you are beginning to learn how helpless you are—and how my love has nothing to do with what you do for me. I love you just as much when you are lying on a sickbed as when you are ministering to others."*

Soon after this the words of a book by Henri Nouwen confirmed this truth to me:

> First of all our life itself is the greatest gift to give—something we constantly forget. When we think about being given to each other, what comes immediately to mind are our unique talents. . . . However, when focusing on talents we tend to forget that our real gift is not so much what we can do but who we are. . . . As I grow older I realize that the greatest gift I have to offer is my own joy of living, my own inner peace, my own silence and solitude, my own sense of well-being.[1]

That's it, I realized. *That's exactly why God is breaking and pruning me. And this is what He has been whispering in my ear ever since I became sick: "It's not your activities, skills, and abilities I want, it's you."*

The lie of society—even Western Christian culture—had fooled me into believing that what we do is more important than who we are. Thus I had come before God, my outstretched hands filled with plans, accomplishments, and abilities to offer Him. Yet as I presented Him the good things I thought made me more acceptable in His sight, He wanted only my empty hands—ready to receive what He chose to give and to do in my life. Only when I relinquished all I had been offering Him to earn His love were my hands finally freed to receive His grace.

Recognizing our struggle with weakness, Craig Barnes writes, "Our needs always provide the opportunity to renew our dependency on the grace of God. What we call need or a 'defect' can become our greatest altar for true worship."[2] As I give Him my "defects," and my limitations, I allow His power to be perfected through me. I no longer need curse my physical limitations, but can accept and even glory in them, for when I am weak, then I am truly strong. Then God uses my weakness to transform me into a vessel for His use, not my own.

Who I am becoming is God's primary concern, not what I can or can't do, as I had so often believed. He loves me not because of what I do, but because He loves me—*He* chose *me*. As I learn to rely solely upon His love and grace, I learn to be still, to cease striving, and to know that He is God (Psalm 46:10). When I embrace my weakness, I find that His grace truly is sufficient.

THE MYSTERY OF LIMITATIONS: REFLECTIONS

QUESTIONS FOR JOURNAL AND/OR SMALL GROUP

1. Are there any good works (activities or accomplishments) with which you seek to dress yourself to become more acceptable to God? to others?
2. What gives you identity apart from God?
3. In what areas of your life do you feel weak or limited? How have you seen God's strength manifested in your weakness or that of others? How might God want to use your limitations to bring Him glory?

4. What might God want to give you if your hands were empty to receive it?

VERSES TO TREASURE

I will glory in my weakness that the power of Christ may dwell in me. (2 Corinthians 12:9, author's paraphrase)

I tried keeping the rules and working my head off to please God, and it didn't work. So I quit . . . so that I could be God's man. It is no longer important that I appear righteous before you or have your good opinion, and I am no longer driven to impress [even] God. Christ lives in me. The life you see me living is not "mine," but it is lived by faith in the Son of God, who loved me and gave himself for me. (Galatians 2:19–20 THE MESSAGE)

In returning and rest you shall be saved, in quietness and trust is your strength. (Isaiah 30:15)

For by grace you have been saved through faith; and not of yourselves, it is a gift of God, not as a result of works, that no one should boast. (Ephesians 2:8–9)

THOUGHTS FOR CONTEMPLATION

"We may desire to bring to the Lord a perfect work. We would like to point, when our work is done, to the beautiful ripened grain and bound-up sheaves; yet the Lord frustrates our plans, shatters our purposes, lets us see the wreck of all our hopes, breaks the beautiful bound structure we thought we were building and catches us up in his arms and whispers to us, 'It's not your work I wanted, but you.' "

—Unknown

"It is not how much we really have to give but how empty we are—so that we can receive fully in our life. Take away your eyes from yourself and rejoice that you have nothing—that you are nothing—that you can do nothing. . . . The more we empty ourselves, the more room we give God to fill us."

—Mother Teresa of Calcutta

HYMN: "Be Still, My Soul"

Be still, my soul—the Lord is on Thy side.
Bear patiently the cross of grief or pain;
Leave to Thy God to order and provide—
In every change He faithful will remain.
Be still, my soul—Thy best, Thy Heavenly Friend
Through thorny ways leads to a joyful end.

Be still, my soul—Thy God doth undertake
To guide the future as He has the past;
Thy hope, Thy confidence let nothing shake—
All now mysterious shall be bright at last.
Be still, my soul—the waves and wind still know
His voice who ruled them while He dwelt below.

Be still, my soul—the hour is hastening on
When we shall be forever with the Lord,
When disappointment, grief, and fear are gone,
Sorrow forgot, love's purest joys restored.
Be still, my soul—when change and tears are past,
All safe and blessed we shall meet at last.

GUIDED MEDITATION: ISAIAH 43:1–4

"But now," says the Lord, your Creator, O Jacob, and He who formed you, O Israel, "Do not fear, for I have redeemed you; I have called you by name; you are mine!"

Hear Him calling your name. Spend time laying each of your fears at His feet. Meditate on His words, "You are mine."

When you pass through the waters, I will be with you; and through the rivers, they will not overflow you.

Imagine yourself in the raging waters of life. God is a life preserver around you, keeping your head above water no matter how high the waves climb. Repeat His promises: "They will not overflow me." Rest in this peace, knowing you are secure even when the crises of life rage loudly and splash over you like waves.

When you walk through the fire you will not be scorched, nor will the flame burn you.

As you feel the heat of trials and pressures all around you, remember that God does not promise we will not feel heat, but that even in its greatest intensity, it will not burn or scorch us. Picture yourself covered from head to toe in fireproof protective wear. Though fire rages all around, you walk through safely because of God's protection covering you.

For I am the Lord your God, the holy One of Israel, your Savior.

Dwell on His character—His faithfulness to His people throughout all of Scripture.

You are precious in My sight. . . . You are honored and I love you.

Repeat these words slowly and meditatively until you truly believe they are spoken to you.

PRAYER

Gracious Lord, there is nothing I can do this day or this year that can compel you to love me more than you already do through your Son, Jesus. Even if I do nothing else from this day forward, your love remains steadfast and fierce over me.

5

TREASURES OF DARKNESS:

THE MYSTERY OF SUFFERING

Darkness shows us worlds of light we never saw by day.
Thomas Moore, 1779–1852

Surely the Lord is in this place, and I did not know it.

Genesis 28:16

WHEN THE UNEXPECTED STRIKES, whether it's loss, brokenness, disappointment, illness, or crisis, we can feel knocked into the cavernous mouth of a deep hole, cast into the blackness of a cave. No longer walking in the light—the known, the norm—we now grope in darkness—the unknown, the uncertain. We wonder when life as we knew it will begin again. As we search for footholds to scale our way out of the chasm, our hands and feet slip down slimy walls. As we call out for answers, only more questions echo back.[1]

When viruses compounding my illness kept me primarily housebound for weeks, and at times even months, the walls of isolation from others—even friends who, healthy and young, could not fully grasp the challenges of living with such limitations—loomed taller and taller. Physically spiraling, emotionally I was caught in the whirlpool sucking me downward. Like David, I cried, "Thou has put me in the lowest pit, in dark places, in the depths. . . . I am shut up and cannot go out" (Psalm 88:6, 8).

THE MYSTERIOUS PATH OF SUFFERING

Around the time of my diagnosis, I had been studying the book of Philippians. When I read the apostle Paul's words, "I want to know Christ and the power of His resurrection," I passionately agreed: *Yes, Lord, I want to know you better!* But as I came to the phrase that followed, "and the fellowship of his sufferings" (3:10), my tongue froze. *Pray for suffering?* The mere idea of suffering made me shudder, let alone the thought of asking for it! Why would Paul pray in this way? I began to wonder if he knew something, perhaps a mystery, or a truth we overlook in our attempts to avoid or quickly get through discomfort.

Though I wanted answers to my questions, though I wanted to be lifted out immediately from the place of darkness and distress, I sensed God was working something much deeper in my life than I could imagine. "Don't run from suffering," Jesus told his disciples. "Embrace it" (Matthew 16:25 THE MESSAGE). The Lord quietly assured me that I was not to fear the valley of suffering—the dark night of the soul—but to welcome it.

Yet as I contemplated facing this darkness, I wrote in my journal: *It has been difficult to allow myself to fully feel the feelings of grief over my loss of health, independence, and relationship with John for fear that they will overwhelm me. I fear that if I embrace them, they will paralyze me.*

Around that time I was also reading an allegory of faith by Hannah Hurnard. In *Hind's Feet on High Places*, a young girl called Much Afraid begins the arduous journey from the Valley of Desolation to the High Places. Alone, afraid, she cries out to the Great Shepherd for help. He lovingly responds by sending her two helpers to guide her. Before seeing them, Much Afraid joyfully expresses her complete confidence in His choosing the best for her.

He then presents the guides: *Sorrow* and *Suffering*.

Petrified by these daunting figures cloaked in dark robes, she turns to the Shepherd and gasps, "I can't go with them! I can't! I can't! O, my Lord, why did you do this to me? It is more than I can bear. . . . Why, oh, why must you make Sorrow and Suffering my companions? Couldn't you have given Joy and Peace to go with me, to strengthen me, and encourage me and help me on the difficult way? I never thought you would do this to me!" And she bursts into tears.

Yet the Great Shepherd chooses these aides precisely for her needs—as He does for us. Though trembling from head to foot at the sight of Sorrow and Suffering, "the two most terrifying things which she could encounter," when Much Afraid looks into the Shepherd's face, she knows she cannot doubt Him. With trembling faith, she slips her hands into theirs.

At the end of the journey, having overcome innumerable trials and temptations to turn back, Much Afraid finally reaches the High Places. The Great Shepherd transforms her difficulties into splendor and gives her a new name, Grace and Glory.

As two brilliantly shining figures approach her, Grace and Glory exclaims, "Oh! You are Suffering and Sorrow!"

They laugh, "Oh, no! We are no more Suffering and Sorrow than you are Much Afraid. . . . Since you brought us here with you, we are turned into *Joy* and *Peace*."

" 'Brought you here?!' " gasped Grace and Glory. "What an extraordinary way to express it! Why, from the first to last you dragged me here."

Again they shook their heads and smiled, "No, we could never have come here alone. Suffering and Sorrow may not enter the Kingdom of Love, but each time you accepted us and put your hands in ours we began to change. Had you turned back or rejected us, we never could have come here."[2]

The apostle James reminds us that the testing of our faith makes us mature and complete (1:2–4). Though I wanted to run like Much Afraid at the sight of dark-cloaked Suffering, I knew God appointed it to strengthen my life. Suffering to the believer works like fertilizer to the seeds of faith. We abhor the stench of manure and, similarly, the agony of pain. However, this very manure, considered waste material, nourishes and feeds the growing fruit of faith and maturity in the garden of our lives. No matter how closely suffering may resemble something worthless, God does not waste any experience in our lives when willingly surrendered to Him. Even Jesus, although He was God's perfect Son, learned obedience from the things He suffered (Hebrews 5:8).

THE GRACE OF SUFFERING

On more difficult days, when sickness kept me in bed, questions began stirring in my mind: *Did I do something to invite this? Is this somehow a sign of God's condemnation of me or of His overlooking me?* Then I came upon a curious verb Paul paired with suffering: "For to you it has been *granted* for Christ's sake, not only to believe in Him, but also to suffer for His sake" (Philippians 1:29). "Granted" implies a gift—something good, something specially selected and lovingly given. Rather than a sign of God's disapproval or neglect, could this adversity, this very thing that has surrounded me in darkness, be a sign of God's movement—even presence—in my life? Rather than punishing or overlooking me, could God be actually *choosing* something for my good, just as the Great Shepherd chose to give Sorrow and Suffering to Much Afraid to guide her?

My pastor once commented, "In God's economy, sometimes the measure of our hurt is the measure of our success." Why? Because suffering makes us more like the Author of our salvation. His allowing us to suffer is a disguised act of grace—the grace of suffering.

I turned to the classic devotional *Streams in the Desert* and read,

> The very fact of trial proves that there is something in us very precious to our Lord; else He would not spend so much pain and time on us. Christ would not test us if He did not see the precious ore of faith mingled in the rocky matrix of our nature; and it is to bring this out into purity and beauty that He forces us through the fiery ordeal.[3]

Whether God himself wounded me, like He did Jacob by the River Jabbok, and the Israelites in the book of Hosea, or whether He merely allowed this affliction, His grace was indeed behind it. And He would use it for good (Genesis 50:20).

STRENGTH FROM SUFFERING

Religious News Service publisher Dale Hanson Bourke describes an interview by an American pastor with a Chinese believer who had been imprisoned ten years for his faith. After the Chinese believer told of the horrible prison conditions, his longing for family members, the sickness and death among prisoners, the American pastor asked his church to pray for an end to persecution in China.

"Oh, no, don't pray for the end of persecution," protested the Chinese Christian. "Suffering has made us strong. It is what has built our faith and caused the underground church to flourish." He then spoke joyfully about the significant spiritual growth among believers in prison and about the many prisoners who'd come to know God.

Bourke reflects, "Most of us are grateful for how little we have suffered. And maybe that's a mistake."[4]

Maybe our attempts to elude suffering are mistakes, as well. Influenced by our culture, which views suffering as something to run from, we often seek whatever ways possible to escape it—denial, drugs, distractions. Suffering doesn't fit with the world's notion of success or with our theology of God's goodness or victorious living in Christ. Jesus often spoke about suffering; yet like Peter and the disciples to whom Christ revealed His imminent anguish and death, we too are tempted to respond, "Oh, that will never happen to you!" (Matthew 16:22).

"The disciples whose thinking is all too earth-bound," writes New Testament scholar Joel Green, "have in mind a powerful Messiah, a life of dominion and glory. They have no room for suffering and martyrdom in their definition of following God."[5] And neither do most of us as twenty-first century Western believers. Our flesh shrinks at the sight of affliction, often desiring happiness over holiness.

In the midst of my struggle to embrace my own suffering, a counselor gave me a Bible study book. Just glancing at the title, *The Way of the Cross*, made me wince. *Ugh*. I didn't want to hear about *that* way. I wanted to hear about the Way of Victory! Or the Way of Triumph! Or the Way of Abundant Life! Or the Way of the Resurrection! But *The Way of the Cross?*

Whether or not I wanted it, the Lord was leading me into the garden of suffering. Several months after my diagnosis, I reflected in my journal:

> *I have entered the garden gate. But this is not a garden of fragrant roses, singing birds, and sunlight on dew-covered grass. This is a garden of darkness, a garden of finitude, a garden of turmoil—the garden that Jesus entered. It is a garden of humanness, of abandonment, of tears. No rays of sunlight shimmer through the trees. No blossoms open their faces to the sun. No birds serenade Him. Rather, in this garden, only the way of the cross beckons Him. And in this dark garden, He waits for me.*

While I journaled about my fear of suffering, I sensed God repond:

> *"If you want to know me better, you must know more suffering—for that is where I have always been. The Pharisees tried to keep me in places of glory so they could be with me there, with people of position and rank. They did all they could to keep me from the tax collectors, the sinners, the lepers, the prostitutes—for Pharisees were not willing to be with them or to be in those places of lowliness, pain, limitations. Even my disciples were quick to want to be with me in glory—'Grant that we may sit with you in glory, on your right and on your left'—but slow to realize that to be with me in glory, they had first to be with me in the cross. Yes, I brought them to glory, but by my way, not theirs."*

Thomas à Kempis (1380–1471) described our aversion to the way of the cross when he wrote,

> Jesus has many who love His Kingdom in Heaven, but few who bear His cross. He has many who desire comfort, but few who desire suffering. He finds many to share His

feast, but few His fasting. All desire to rejoice with Him, but few are willing to suffer for His sake. Many follow Jesus to the breaking of the bread, but few to the drinking of the cup of His Passion.[6]

THE TREASURE OF SUFFERING

As another year passed, though I knew God was teaching me much through suffering, I grew tired of the struggles and wanted to push away the cup. "Enough, Lord!" I wanted to say. "Haven't I been pruned enough for a while?" How desperately I longed for Him to deliver me from the trials, to bring restoration of the losses—health, vocation, finances, relationship, dreams—I had endured. If God was God, He *could* do that, right? If He was loving, He *would* do that, right? How tempted I was to believe that if God truly cared about me, and if He was all-powerful, He would dispel the darkness and pull me from the pit.

Yet as I continued praying in the dark, I stumbled upon a treasure. While I had been praying that He deliver me from the suffering by healing my body and spirit, He instead offered me something better—something I would have easily missed had I insisted upon immediate restoration as the sign of His love. More often than not, God *doesn't* remove our suffering or even change our circumstances. He does something greater: *He enters into our suffering with us.* The Lord Jesus enters into the fullness of our pain, here and now, and bears it with us.

Through the loneliest and sickest nights, when I had not even the strength to pray, I experienced a special intimacy with Christ in a manner I had previously not known. I finally understood why Paul prayed to know Christ and the fellowship of His sufferings. The journey to know Christ better winds through the depths: "Though I walk through the valley of darkness, I will not fear for thou art with me" (Psalm 23:4, author's paraphrase). If we seek a detour around it, we forfeit a chance to walk alongside the Suffering Servant. In order to know Christ more intimately, to more fully identify with Him, I must share in His sufferings by experiencing suffering myself. As He wept in the Garden alone, facing His cup of suffering, He tenderly holds me—and even weeps with me—as I face mine. "In all their affliction, He was afflicted" (Isaiah 63:9).

Two people who have endured similar pain (death of a child, divorce, cancer) share an indescribable bond. Likewise, our affliction, whatever the nature, forges a deeper intimacy between ourselves and Christ, the Suffering Servant. Nothing—not healing, not restoration, not success—compares with the comfort and sweetness of this fellowship.

The more valuable an owner's treasure, the farther into the darkness of a cave or pit he will bury it. Like diamonds excavated from mines, the costliest gems lie hidden far from the light of day. The greatest treasure I have found in the darkness—the "Hope" diamond—is deepened intimacy and identity with Christ as I fellowship in His sufferings.

GOD IS IN THE DARK

When we are willing to embrace the suffering and darkness—the place where it appears God is farthest away—we find He is actually there. God is in the dark!

In his sermon "Listening to the Dark," Eugene Lowry reflects on God speaking to Elijah in his despair (1 Kings 19):

> In the midst of the darkness of the cave finally came this voice. The voice came up close to the ear and whispered. And the voice said, "What are you doing here?"
>
> That's one of the most remarkable passages in all of Scripture. What do you mean, "What are you doing *here*?" Do you notice what the voice did not say? It did not say, "What are you doing *there*"—as though God were distant and aloof, looking on to the scene of the cave saying, "What are you doing there, Elijah? Why are you there?" We're not talking *there*; we're talking *here*.

God is in the dark. In fact, God is bigger than the dark. God is the Creator of the dark. And the promise is that God will be present.[7]

Yes, *God* is the One forming light and creating darkness (Isaiah 45:7). God is the One who does not merely check in on us in the darkness, but who *abides* with us in the darkness. When Jacob, fleeing from his brother Esau, spent the night alone in the wilderness, God showed Jacob His presence in a dream. Jacob awoke and said, "Surely the Lord is in this place, and I did not know it" (Genesis 28:16).

God not only abides with us in the dark, He is at *work* in the dark. When we cannot understand, we can take courage that God *is* indeed moving. God is doing something wondrous, something glorious.

A. W. Tozer observed,

> It is heartening to learn how many of God's mighty deeds were done in secret, away from the prying eyes of men or angels. When God created the heavens and the earth, darkness was upon the face of the deep. When the eternal Son became flesh, He was carried for a time in the darkness of the sweet virgin's womb. When He died for the life of the world, it was in the darkness, seen by no one at the last. When He arose from the dead, it was "very early in the morning." No one saw Him rise. It is as if God were saying, "What I am is all that need matter to you, for therein lies your hope and your peace. I will do what I will do, and it will all come to light at last, but how I do it is My secret. Trust Me, and be not afraid."[8]

In the darkness—of Gethsemane, of Mary's womb, of the cross, of the garden tomb—God's deepest work is done. Darkness is the locus of death—and of new life. In the dark earth where none can see, where all seems dead, lost, barren, the seed of new life germinates. We need not fear this place, for in the darkness the most valuable treasures, and God, await us. "I will give you the treasures of darkness, and hidden wealth of secret places, in order that you may know that it is I, the Lord" (Isaiah 45:3).

We have no guarantees our lives in this fallen world will be free from suffering. In fact, Scripture teaches that believers will likely face more suffering than most people. Many followers of Christ hurt deeply, and thousands are persecuted around the world today. We have no guarantees that hardships will pass quickly, that we will be delivered from pain, or that others will understand. But there is one guarantee: God is with us in the dark. And that is enough.

The Enemy of our souls tempts us to believe that suffering is negative, a sign of God's neglect or of our own failure, thus convincing us to avoid suffering (and sadly, sometimes evade those we know who are struggling). He knows that suffering is one of the greatest means to draw us closer to Jesus and to teach us increasing dependence upon Him. Thus he will do whatever it takes to have us run from it . . . until God, in His grace, allows trials from which we cannot run. When Peter refuses to accept Jesus' imminent passion, Jesus responds, "Get behind Me, Satan!" (Matthew 16:23). We can do the same.

Trials, hardships, and adversity are more the norm of this life than the abnorm. In fact, when my life was relatively free of hardship, how easy it was to find comfort in this earthly home. Yet suffering stimulates our hunger for heaven, our real home, where Jesus will wipe away every tear. We can say with the apostle Paul's confidence, "For I consider that the sufferings of this present time are not worthy to be compared with the glory that is to be revealed to us" (Romans 8:18).

IN THE GARDEN

We wait for the time and place when life will be how God intended it in the beginning: perfect, sweet fellowship with Him in the Garden of Paradise. There we will know and love Him absolutely and completely. Until Christ takes us home to walk in unbroken communion, we can fellowship with Him in the other Garden: Gethsemane, the Garden of suffering and tears. We need not fear entering that Garden, for Jesus is already there, waiting for us in the dark of the night. And He reaches out to welcome us with hands that bear the scars of suffering—and palms on which our names are inscribed (Isaiah 49:16).

THE MYSTERY OF SUFFERING: REFLECTIONS

QUESTIONS FOR JOURNAL AND/OR SMALL GROUP

1. Scripture often uses metaphors to describe the emotional or spiritual place one is in, such as the valley of darkness, or a pit, or the depths. What image can you use to describe to God how you feel?
2. Read Psalm 88. What portion do you most relate to? What encourages you?
3. What "fruit" has been developed in your life as a result of the fertilizer of trials and suffering?
4. Write your own psalm or poem to God.
5. From Scripture, memorize a promise about suffering.

PROMISES TO CLAIM IN DARKNESS

For Thou dost light my lamp; the Lord God illumines my darkness. (Psalm 18:28)

I will make darkness into light before them and crooked places straight. (Isaiah 42:16)

If I say, "Surely the darkness will overwhelm me, and the light around me will be night," even the darkness is not dark to

Thee and the night is as bright as the day. Darkness and light are alike to Thee. (Psalm 139:11–12)

In all their affliction He was afflicted, and the angel of His presence saved them; and He lifted them and carried them all the days of old. (Isaiah 63:9)

He brought them out of darkness and the deepest gloom and broke away their chains. (Psalm 107:14 NIV)

The Lord will command his lovingkindness in the daytime; and His song will be with me in the night. (Psalm 42:8)

PRAYING THE PSALMS

"Since I am afflicted and needy, let the Lord be mindful of me; Thou art my help and my deliverer; do not delay, O my God" (Psalm 40:17).

"Turn to me and be gracious to me, for I am lonely and afflicted. The troubles of my heart are enlarged; bring me out of my distresses" (Psalm 25:16–17).

"Return, O Lord, rescue my soul; save me because of Thy lovingkindness. . . . I am weary with my sighing; every night I make my bed swim, I dissolve my couch with my tears" (Psalm 6:4, 6).

"O God, do not be far from me, O my God, hasten to my help! . . . Thou, who hast shown me many troubles and distresses, wilt revive me again, and wilt bring me up again from the depths of the earth. Mayest Thou increase my greatness, and turn to comfort me" (Psalm 71:12, 20–21).

THOUGHTS FOR CONTEMPLATION

"Nothing therefore, happens, unless the Omnipotent wills it to happen; He either permits it to happen, or he brings it about himself."

—St. Augustine of Hippo

"He watches over me in such a way that not a hair can fall from my head without the will of my Father in heaven: in fact all things must work together for my salvation. . . . All things come to us, not by chance, but from his fatherly hand."

—*Heidelberg Catechism*

"Never shrink from deep devotion because you fear its trials and sacrifices. Paul in martyrdom was unspeakably happier than God's half-hearted servants."

—William Huntington, c. 1870

"Suffering is the highest action of Christian obedience, and I call blessed not those who have worked, but all who have suffered. Suffering is the greatest work in the discipleship of Jesus."

—Herman Bezzel, *Pastoralblatter*

"There is no pit so deep that God's love is not deeper still."

—Corrie ten Boom, Holocaust survivor

HYMN: "It Is Well With My Soul"

After the death of his four daughters in a shipwreck, Horatio G. Spafford sailed across the ocean to meet his wife, who was traveling with their children when they died. Passing over the spot where his daughters perished, he wept. He then returned to his cabin, picked up his pen, and began to write "It Is Well With My Soul."

When peace like a river attendeth my way,
When sorrows like sea billows roll—
Whatever my lot, Thou hast taught me to say,
"It is well, it is well with my soul."

Though Satan should buffet, though trials should come,
Let this blessed assurance control,
That Christ hath regarded my helpless estate,
And hath shed His own blood for my soul.

And Lord, haste the day when faith shall be made sight,

The clouds be rolled back like a scroll:
The trump shall resound and the Lord shall descend,
Even so—it is well with my soul.

THE TAPESTRY

Then shall I know . . .
not till the loom is silent
and the shuttles cease to fly,
Shall God unroll the canvas
and explain the reason why.
The dark threads are as needful
in the weaver's skillful hand,
As the threads of gold and silver
in the pattern He has planned.

—Unknown

GUIDED MEDITATION: SELECTIONS FROM PSALM 40

I waited patiently for the Lord.

Take time to sit in silence before Him, quieting your thoughts, your body, and your emotions.

He inclined to me, and heard my cry.

Picture a patient, gentle father bending down to comfort his crying child. Take time to pour your heart out to God.

He brought me up out of the pit of destruction, out of the miry clay.

Feel yourself being lifted from the chasm of darkness toward the light; feel your feet being gently pulled from the sticky clay.

He set my feet upon a rock making my footsteps firm.

Allow God—not your striving, wriggling, or pushing—to set your feet upon the Rock of His strength. Feel how stable your feet are upon the flat, solid granite beneath you. Look at the beautiful view.

He put a new song in my mouth, a song of praise to our God.

Ask the Lord to give you a "song in the night." Let His Spirit bring to mind a song you know, or lead you to make up one as you sing to Him. Picture Him taking your words of worry and fret and replacing them with a song of praise in your mouth. Sing those praises to Him.

Many will see and fear, and will trust in the Lord.

Pray that through even this trial in your life, many *will* see and fear and trust in the Lord.

Thou, O Lord, will not withhold thy compassion from me; thy lovingkindness and thy truth will continually preserve me.

Envision shields of His compassion, lovingkindness, and truth protecting and sustaining you.

Since I am afflicted and needy, let the Lord be mindful of me; Thou art my help and my deliverer; do not delay, O my God.

Thank Him that He is with you and ever mindful of you. Express your trust in Him that He will deliver you at the right time. Ask that He be glorified in the midst of this darkness.

PRAYER

Thank you, Lord, for this garden of suffering—for this germination time. Though I would rather behold a bed of bright yellow daffodils, perfumed roses, or sweet strawberries, let me not disdain this period of waiting—this time when I see no signs of growth, new life, or movement of your hand.

Lord, I believe—I choose to believe—when I do not see, that beneath the surface, invisible to my eye, buried in the damp, dark, dense earth, life grows! Transformation occurs! Your work, vital work, root work—which gives daffodils their vibrant color, roses their delightful fragrance, strawberries their succulent flavor—pulsates in the black soil.

O God, may I not look each morning for a sign of new life—an ending to the pain and the dark place—and when seeing none, stomp off in frustration and anger at you. Or sulk in doubt and despair. When you toss fertilizer on me, help me to not cringe at the stench of adversity and suffering, but welcome this essential food for my growth.

May I praise you even when there is no blossom on the tree or fruit on the vine (Habakkuk 3:17), because I know that you are a God of mystery. You are the One who takes my lifeless seed and plunges it into the darkness of the deep earth.

If I cry to be lifted from this place void of light, plead to be brought into the fresh air where I could have room to bend and sway, I would merely be asking for death of the roots that you have begun. My little seed beginning to sprout life would wither upon the sun-baked soil, exposed to burning heat and preying birds. My flowers would have no fragrance to perfume the earth or vibrant color to offer beauty, and my fruit no flesh to feed a hungry soul. And the work you have begun in me would quickly dry up and blow away.

Blessed is the man who trusts in the Lord and whose trust is the Lord. For he will be like a tree planted by the water, that extends its roots by a stream and will not fear when the heat comes. But its leaves will be green, and it will not be anxious in a year of drought nor cease to yield fruit. (Jeremiah 17:7–8)

6

A DAY IN HIS COURTS:

THE MYSTERY OF SOLITUDE AND SILENCE

We need silence to be alone with God, to speak to Him, to listen to Him, to ponder His words deep in our hearts. We need to be alone with God in silence to be renewed and to be transformed. . . . In the silence of our hearts He will speak to us, if we stop talking and give Him a chance. . . .

The more we receive in our silent prayer, the more we can give in our active life. Silence gives us a new way of looking at everything. We need this silence in order to touch souls. The essential thing is not what we say but what God says to us and what He says through us.

Mother Teresa of Calcutta

A day in Thy courts is better than a thousand outside.

Psalm 84:10

I TURN MY CAR OFF the highway as cars whir past. Gravel crunches under my tires as I slowly ascend the 1 1/2-mile driveway leading to the monastery perched a thousand feet above the shore. The Pacific Ocean stretches endlessly below, the sun radiates above, and a family of rabbits hops across the winding road before me.

Something bid me here to Immaculate Heart Hermitage. Was I crazy? Three years had passed since I first noticed symptoms of sickness, and I had recently recuperated from another long bout fighting a virus. Just as I had started to feel better, a friend who had to move unexpectedly called and offered me her apartment in San Francisco rent-free until her lease expired. Her offer seemed the perfect opportunity to live on my own again while not strong enough to work full-time. I could feel—or pretend to feel—like any other healthy and independent person my age.

JESUS' JOURNEY INTO SOLITUDE

However, just after my friend's phone call—during the first days of Lent—I read in Matthew's gospel about Jesus being led by the Spirit into the desert for forty days. Alone. Though I'd spent significant time by myself over the past few years when sick, something about Jesus' experience tugged at me. I recalled a section from a book by Henri Nouwen that another friend had lent me:

In the lonely place Jesus finds the courage to follow God's will and not his own; to speak God's words and not his own; to do God's work and not his own. He reminds us constantly: "I can do nothing by myself . . . my aim is to do not my own will, but the will of Him who sent me" (John 5:30). It is in the lonely place, where Jesus enters into *intimacy with the Father*, that his ministry is born.[1]

The more I prayed about it, the more solitude became like a magnetic force pulling me away from jumping at the chance to live in San Francisco. The whispered invitation to cultivate deeper intimacy with the Father through solitude beckoned me.

During the darkness of suffering, silence had chosen me. Now I found *I* was choosing *it*. My broken, formerly self-reliant spirit could now begin healing in the cast of Solitude and Silence. As uncomfortable as that cast appeared—and as hard as it was to forsake an attractive opportunity to feel independent and "normal"—strapped close to the Father's chest in the sling of stillness, I knew I could better hear His heartbeat and learn to rest upon Him.

In *Out of Solitude*, Nouwen notes,

> Jesus went to a lonely place to pray, that is, to grow in the awareness that all the power he had was *given* to him; that all the words he spoke came from the Father; and that all the works he did were not really his but the works of the One who had sent Him. . . . It is in this solitude that *being* is more important than *having*, and that we are worth more than the result of our efforts. . . . In solitude we become aware that our *worth* is not the same as our *use-fulness*.[2]

Jesus journeyed into solitude, compelled not by drivenness to accomplish great works or to prove His significance, but by the Spirit of God (Matthew 4:1). Satan offered Jesus tantalizing temptations in the desert to make a name for himself. But Jesus' only ambition was to listen to and obey the Father; He did nothing on His own initiative (John 5:30). Instead of seeking to be *useful*, He entered into solitude to *listen* to the Father, and from this His ministry emerged. I longed for Jesus' ambition to become mine.

No longer toiling to produce results from my own striving

efforts, I came to the monastery to water seeds of stillness through solitude and silence and let Jesus, the Vine, do the work of bearing fruit: "I am the vine, you are the branches; he who abides in Me, and I in him, he bears much fruit. . . . Apart from Me you can do nothing" (John 15:5).

Though what lay beyond the walls of the monastery was a mystery to me, I knew I had much to learn from those practiced in the disciplines of silence, solitude, and listening.

LEARNING FROM MONKS

"Hello, Stacey," Brother Joshua, the official "greeter" monk, welcomed me. Wearing a white terry cloth fisherman's cap, dark sunglasses, and blue jeans, he didn't look anything like the hermit monk I had pictured, nor much like the other monks, who were clothed from head to toe in their brown habits. He led me down a narrow dirt path to my little trailer cabin named DOXA ("Glory"), overlooking the Pacific. Strolling onto the front porch, I inhaled delicious coastal air and basked in the thought of three weeks here. No traffic, no phone, no mail, no computer, no television—just morning greetings from blue jays on my deck, noon visits from foxes rummaging for lunch scraps, and evening entertainment from a million glittering stars.

I began recording thoughts each day in my journal:

DAY 3: *So far no earth-shattering spiritual revelations have come to me. Wouldn't it be wonderful if all one had to do was travel to a monastery for a few days to really "hear God"?*

Coming to seek solitude, I thought I'd made significant strides in cultivating the practice of silence. Apart from a little cabin fever during a three-day downpour, I enjoyed alone time—interspersed with chats with the sprightly gardener from England. Yet even days spent mostly in silence did not expose the noise in my soul as did meditating with the monks.

DAY 4: *As I have been doing the last few nights, I joined the monks for their evening Vespers service in which they chant the Psalms. Yet this time I decided to follow them into the meditation sanctuary to see what they do. After entering the candle-lit circular room beside the main chapel and gathering in a circle, the monks settle into a cross-legged sitting position on the floor as easily as most men plop down on a couch to watch Monday night football.*

Dong! The abbot strikes the metal gong, signaling the beginning of meditation. Stillness hovers over us, and no one appears to move. I feel like a squirmy child waiting impatiently for her "time out" to end. Many minutes pass before I can even begin to focus upon being still. I swish my tongue over my teeth, removing the sweet-potato remnants from dinner. Deep spiritual thoughts fill my mind . . . Hmmm. What spice was that the cook used? It would go well with chicken. I remember the unfinished projects on my desk at home, the birthday card I forgot to send, the smog appointment I must make for my car.

Stillness!

A minute later, I feel an itch in my nose. Prickly sensations creep up my left foot as it starts to fall asleep. I want to move, stretch my legs, stand up, sing a song, anything other than sit completely still in utter silence for what seems like hours. While readjusting my position, I discreetly gaze at my watch. Only six minutes have passed!

Until now, I rather prided myself on being here three days and hardly feeling restless or bored. I assumed I'd adapted to silence and solitude quite easily. I loved returning to my cozy cabin without seeing a little red light blinking on an answering machine, feeling the urge to check my e-mail, sorting through junk mail, or rushing to my next appointment. But as I sit in meditation, the silence exposes my restless spirit. I want to dart out of there, but no one seems to make a move. As time creeps on, I want to raise my hand and say, "Excuse me? Can we go now?"

A few more minutes pass, and I dream about jumping up and exclaiming: "Let's go, guys. Time's up. Move 'em out! Vamanos!*" But they continue—totally unaware of the torture this stillness is causing my type-A personality. After what feels like five hours,* Dong—*the abbot strikes the gong, marking the end of our thirty-minute meditation. I quietly follow them out and sigh with relief in the crisp evening air.*

Meditation—oh, to practice it daily! Why is such a seemingly simple exercise so excruciatingly challenging? One that brings so much up in my soul—angst, fear, boredom, frustration, delight, worry. These all dance about on the stage of my mind as I try to quiet the audience of my thoughts in preparation to hear God.

LISTENING WITH THE SOUL

Why is listening so hard? Why is silence so mysterious, unsettling, even scary? I'd spent time reading, writing, thinking, praying, dreaming—all wonderful, quiet activities—but as I was honest with myself, I realized I hadn't waited before God to listen for longer than two minutes. Silence reveals the chatter of my soul: my anxiety, my impatience, my lack of trust, my motives, and my selfish ambitions. In silence, I am no longer in control. Talking enables me to defend, justify, and explain myself. But silence requires me simply to *be* before God, to let Him do the talking.

John Leax wrote of his experience in solitude at a monastery:

Nothing prepared me for this silence. I expected an absence of sound. I am overwhelmed by a positive presence. The solitude I feel is a new thing, entirely unlike the solitude of the mountains or the river. It is a terrible confrontation with the noisiness of my own soul and mind. I want to make a noise, go introduce myself to the man down the hall. If I could talk about God, I wouldn't have to face Him. But here in this silence, all the talking is done by God.[3]

When God talks, I don't always want to hear Him, though I say I do. I am uncomfortable with hearing words of conviction and even words of love—love lavished upon me apart from anything I have done or plan to do for Him. When I fall short of faithfully being the person I know I am called to be, I feel less than lovable. Receiving His words of grace and affection can be painfully difficult. Like an uncomely peasant girl who withdraws in shame at the beckoning words of love from a handsome prince, we, too, are sometimes afraid to hear the powerful whispers of delight and acceptance from our great King.

Yet in silence I learn that listening is just as important a part of prayer as speaking. Perhaps more so. The writer of Ecclesiastes admonishes us:

> Guard your steps as you go to the house of God, and draw near to listen rather than to offer the sacrifice of fools. . . . Do not be hasty in word or impulsive in thought to bring up a matter in the presence of God. For God is in heaven and you are on the earth; therefore, let your words be few. (5:1–2)

In deep conversation with a friend or spouse, we put down the paper, turn off the TV, face them, and look into their eyes. Likewise, we must position ourselves to hear God. Habakkuk states, "I will stand on my guard post and station myself on the rampart; and I will keep watch to see what He will speak to me" (2:1). Positioning requires setting aside that which keeps us from listening—or setting ourselves in a place where we can better listen.

A poster I once saw showed a little girl at the beach looking intently toward the ocean. The words beneath the scene read, *"The polite part of speaking with God is waiting long enough to listen."* My often-used excuse for not doing so—"I'm too busy"—is, in truth, "I'm afraid." Afraid at times of hearing His love and not having earned it; afraid at other times of not hearing anything. Sitting at God's feet with no agenda feels frightening.

Influenced by our productivity-driven culture, we want to walk away from our time with God holding some tangible result. The incessant noise and activity of our 24/7 lifestyle affects not only our daily lives but also our spiritual lives. A. W. Tozer noted,

> This is definitely not the hour when men will take kindly to an exhortation to listen, for listening is not today a part of popular religion. . . . Religion has accepted the monstrous heresy that noise, size, activity, and bluster make a man dear to God.[4]

Buying the cultural lie, we begin to evaluate our worldly as well as our spiritual success by what we produce. Who has time to listen when there are so many *important* things to be done? Afraid of wasting time, we miss out on the pure delight of simply being with God. Yes, God wants to hear our concerns. Yet like a loving father, He desires His children to come to Him not only with requests but also with the desire simply to *be* with Him. Like a father who delights when his child comes to curl up on his lap, play horsey, or walk together hand in hand, God wants us to enjoy Him for who He is, not merely what He does for us.

"One of the first things a spiritual pilgrim must learn," wrote Christian mystic Jeanne Guyon, "is to be quiet before God and to remain before Him—coming without any request or even any personal will in any matter."[5] As two lovers are content to simply be in each other's presence, not needing always to speak, God delights for us to be still before Him, savoring His presence. He yearns for our devotion and grieves when we are "led astray from the simplicity and purity of devotion to Christ" (2 Corinthians 11:3).

Though meditating with the monks that first night felt like Chinese water torture, something led me back the next evening.

I wrote in my journal before going: *What a funny thing about meditation. Everything in my natural way of functioning is averse to it, but I am deeply drawn to it. It's terribly uncomfortable, yet, I suspect, immensely freeing.*

> DAY 5: *Again I sit in the circle. Again I squirm. Again I peer through the dim light at the cloaked figures in complete stillness around me. These monks seem not only oblivious to me, but also to the noise of the outside world chanting mantras of "go, go, go," "do, do, do," "busy, busy, busy."*
>
> *How do they make it look so easy? Is this really worth the time? What does it accomplish, anyway? Shouldn't I be doing something productive? As my mind begins churning with these protests, the words of Jesus break through:* Peace. Be still (Mark 4:39 NRSV).
>
> *Repeating His words,* Peace. Be still *silently with each breath, a breeze of peace fills my soul. Jesus, as He spoke to the wind-whipped Sea of Galilee, making it perfectly calm, speaks to my fretful sea of thoughts, calming the waves of worry with His word.*

PRIORITIES FROM SILENCE

As I enter into the mystery of solitude, I discover that my most significant work emerges not from noise and activity but from silent waiting upon God. Meister Eckhart, a thirteenth-century mystic, observed, "The outward will never be puny if the inward work is great."

Yet our tendency, like the Israelites, is to focus on the outward, the active. Isaiah says to the frantic children of God, *In repentance and rest you shall be saved; in quietness and trust is your strength* (Isaiah 30:15). They replied, *"No, for we will flee on horses"* (v. 16).

We, too, resist God's call to quietness and trust, choosing instead to jump on horses of busyness and self-reliance in our race toward significance. Solitude and silence call us to lay down the reins of control and, as did King David, wait upon God to save us: *My soul waits in silence for God only; from Him is my salvation.* (Psalm 62:1)

Far from being a waste of time, silence and solitude enable us to discern *God's* priorities for our time. Thomas Merton, a monk greatly experienced in the practice of silence, observed, "In silence, we learn to make distinctions."[6] Silence enables us to distinguish between God's still, small voice and the shouts of the world.

Throughout His ministry, Jesus often stole away to a quiet place to commune with God. He also instructed His disciples— and us—to "come away by yourselves to a lonely place and rest a while" (Mark 6:31). After spending a long day ministering to the sick, demon-possessed, blind, and downtrodden, Jesus awoke early the next morning. While it was still dark, He went off in solitude to pray and to listen to the Father (Mark 1:35). Had He not done this, perhaps He would have been persuaded to return to the same village the next day to minister to the needs of even greater crowds that had formed. For meeting the needs of those who'd come to Him was what He should do, wasn't it? How could He move on to another village when such great needs surrounded Him?

In the gospel of Mark, we read,

> The disciples searched for him [he obviously had withdrawn quite a distance in solitude] and when they found him they stated, "Everybody is looking for you." He answered, "Let us go elsewhere to the neighboring country towns so I can preach there too, because that is what I came out for. (1:36–38)

Jesus could move on, even in the face of unmet needs, because he let neither the crowds nor his disciples—only time alone with the Father—define what he should do. Quaker writer Thomas Kelly recognized the importance of receiving our call from God, rather than those around us:

> Much of our acceptance of multitudes of obligations is due to our inability to say No. We calculated that that task had to be done, and we saw no one ready to undertake it. We calculated the need, and then calculated our time, and decided maybe we could squeeze it in somewhere. But the decision was a heady decision, not made within the sanctuary of the soul. When we say Yes or No to calls for service on the basis of heady decisions, we have to give reasons, to ourselves and to others. But when we say Yes or No to calls on the basis of inner guidance and whispered promptings of encouragement from the Center of our life, or [in the case of No] on the basis of a lack of any inward "rising" of that Life to encourage us in the call, we have no reason to give, except one—the will of God as we discern it.[7]

DAY 8: *Night after night, as I practice meditative silence, I find myself increasingly drawn to it. With each half-hour session, the itches in my feet and running to-do list in my mind lose their power to disturb me. And I begin to listen.*

Silence and solitude, like the prongs on a tuning fork, enable us to discern the sound of God's voice. The more we tune our ears to His tone, the better we can discern what *isn't* His voice. The Enemy's once-seducing whispers of doubt, condemnation, and fear begin to sound clearly off pitch.

On my first evening at the monastery, I wrote in my journal,

> *One might think that coming to a monastery, even for three weeks, would require giving up so much. But what I realize sitting here tonight in quiet is, I have given up nothing—nothing, that is, but restlessness, activity, busyness, and striving. I have gained everything—everything that is important to me—especially being with God. It is so*

wonderful to be. Yet how can I simply be when back in a world that calls us to forever do?

On my last day, as I drove down the gravel road toward the highway, I knew a busy world sped before me. Yet after three weeks at the hermitage, I learned that silence, not a monastery, is the answer. Cultivating intimacy with the Father in a place of solitude—whether that be in a corner of my house, on a park bench, on a stroll through the woods, at a retreat center, or even in my car—enables me, like Jesus, to align my priorities with God, to follow His will and not my own. The road to quiet and calm is not simply escaping the outer noise (phone, mail, traffic, to-do lists); it's allowing God to quiet inner noise as I sit at His feet. Though I may appear to be wasting time, in silence and solitude I allow my agenda to be shaped by the only One existing outside of time... the One who holds my times in His hands (Psalm 31:15).

In the mystery of solitude and silence, I discover that my willingness to be "useless"—unproductive—enables me to be truly useful to God. For it's in silence, not activity, that my deepest, most significant work emerges.

THE MYSTERY OF SOLITUDE AND SILENCE: REFLECTIONS

QUESTIONS FOR JOURNAL AND/OR SMALL GROUP

1. What keeps you from making time for silence or solitude? What fears might keep you from silence?
2. Schedule an hour of silence and solitude sometime this week as you plan other appointments. Try also to schedule a day or half-day this month. See the Epilogue for ideas on planning a longer retreat.

3. Mahatma Gandhi said, "God speaks to us every day, only we don't know how to listen." How could you practice listening throughout today?

VERSES TO TREASURE

Incline your ear and come to Me. Listen that you may live. (Isaiah 55:3)

The Lord is good to those who wait for Him, to the person who seeks Him. It is good that he waits silently. . . . Let him sit alone and be silent. (Lamentations 3:25–26, 28)

Be still before the Lord and wait patiently for Him. (Psalm 37:7 NIV)

Pay attention to Me, O My people; and give ear to Me. . . . Listen to Me. (Isaiah 51:4; 49:1)

The Lord is in His holy temple. Let all the earth be silent before Him. (Habakkuk 2:20)

THOUGHTS FOR CONTEMPLATION

"It is seldom that our silence and our prayers do more to bring people to the knowledge of God than all our words about Him. The mere fact that you wish to give God glory by talking about Him is no proof that your speech will give Him glory. What if He should prefer you to be silent? Have you never heard that silence gives Him glory?"

—Thomas Merton, *No Man Is an Island*

"A hearing heart depends upon an utter willingness to obey, the whole time, in tiny details as well as big ones. In Hebrew, an 'obedient heart' is the same word as a 'hearing heart.' If one hears the voice of God it should mean obedience, and if one obeys one will hear."

—Hannah Hurnard, *The Hearing Heart*

"A man prayed, and at first he thought that prayer was talking. But he became more and more quiet until in the end he realized that prayer is listening."

—Søren Kierkegaard, *Christian Discourses*

EXERCISE IN *LECTIO DIVINA**

1. To begin, choose a passage in Scripture approximately five to eight verses in length, shorter if the verses are long (for example, Isaiah 43:1–3). Whether alone or in a group, choose a quiet atmosphere where you can be silent to meditate and listen.

Start by asking the Spirit of God to guide your thoughts and keep your mind on His Word. (Distractions will come, but continue returning to the text when you catch your mind wandering.) Ask Him to silence all voices and thoughts that are not from Him.

Take a few moments to quiet your thoughts. As you take some deep breaths, breathe out worries and preoccupations; breathe in God's peace.

2. Slowly read the passage aloud, twice. Listen for a word or phrase that particularly strikes you. Take a minute to focus upon the word by repeating it silently and meditatively. In group *lectio*, after this minute, each participant shares the word that struck him or her, without offering any explanation or commentary. Everyone in the group listens.

Slowly read the passage aloud again. This time be aware of an image or picture that comes to mind, or a feeling that you experience. In group *lectio*, share that image or feeling.

3. Open yourself to whatever God may be inviting you through the passage to do.

Read the passage once more aloud (or silently, if alone). If

Lectio Divina is Latin for "divine [or holy] reading." For centuries it has been practiced by believers as a means of deepening one's experience with Scripture and God through meditative reading and listening. It can be practiced in small groups or individually.

you prefer variety, you may want to use another version of the Bible, such as *The Message*.

Consider: What might God be asking me through His Word to do today?

4. Pray: Ask God to help you do what He has spoken. Take time to rest in His presence, entrusting all you have heard to Him. In group *lectio*, pray for the person on your right that he or she would respond to God's invitation.

FURTHER THOUGHTS FOR CONTEMPLATION

"The simplest and oldest way in which God manifests Himself is through and in the earth itself. And He still speaks to us through the earth and sea, the birds of the air and the little living creatures upon the earth, if we can but *quiet ourselves to listen*."

—Richard Foster, *Celebration of Discipline*

Take some time this week in solitude in nature to listen to God through His creation—a walk through a rose garden, sitting by a pond or lake, an evening stroll under starlight, getting up to see the sunrise.

PRAYER OF A. W. TOZER

"Lord, teach me to listen. The times are noisy and my ears are weary with the thousand raucous sounds that continuously assault them. Give me the spirit of the boy Samuel when he said to Thee, 'Speak, for thy servant heareth.' Let me hear Thee speaking in my heart. Let me get used to the sound of Thy Voice, that its tones may be familiar when the sounds of earth die away and the only sound will be the music of Thy speaking Voice. Amen."

PRAYER OF HENRI NOUWEN

"O Lord Jesus, your words to your Father were born out of your silence. Lead me into this silence, so that my words may be

spoken in your name and thus fruitful. It is so hard to be silent, silent with my mouth, but even more, silent with my heart. There is so much talking going on within me. It seems that I am always involved in inner debates with my friends, my enemies, my colleagues, my rivals, and myself. But this inner debate reveals how far my heart is from you. If I were simply to rest at your feet and realize that I belong to you and you alone, I would easily stop arguing with all the real and imagined people around me. These arguments show my insecurity, my fear, my apprehensions, and my need for being recognized and receiving attention. You, O Lord, will give me all the attention I need if I would simply stop talking and start listening to you. I know that in the silence of my heart you will speak to me and show me your love. Give me, O Lord, that silence. Let me be patient and grow slowly into this silence in which I can be with you. Amen."

RECOMMENDED BOOKS

Brother Lawrence. *The Practice of the Presence of God*. Mt. Vernon, N.Y.: Peter Pauper Press, 1963.

Foster, Richard. *Celebration of Discipline*. New York: Harper & Row, 1978.

Jones, Timothy. *A Place for God: A Guide to Spiritual Retreat Centers*. New York: Image Books (Doubleday), n.d.

Norris, Kathleen. *The Cloister Walk*. New York: Riverhead Books, 1996.

Nouwen, Henri. *Out of Solitude*. South Bend, Ind.: Ave Maria Press, 1974.

Willard, Dallas. *The Spirit of the Disciplines*. New York: HarperCollins Publishers, 1991.

7

LIVING WITH UNFULFILLED LONGINGS:

THE MYSTERY OF DESIRE

The whole life of the good Christian is a holy longing.
St. Augustine of Hippo

Whom have I in heaven but Thee? And besides Thee, I desire nothing on earth.

Psalm 73:25

WALKING INTO THE brightly painted nursery with my longtime friend, I watched her two-year-old daughter run and jump into her arms with delight, shouting, "Mommy! Mommy!" The joy on their faces paralleled the hidden pain in my heart. I turned my face to conceal my unexpected tears.

When, Lord? I cried silently.

Though normally filled with gladness when watching my friends with their children, for some reason that morning I was overwhelmed with sadness in longing for a little girl to call me "Mommy." As much as I tried to shake my emotion, I couldn't.

When will I—or will I ever—have a family? I wondered. Though God graciously had given me much joy and contentment as a single person, I still desired to have a family—a longing that only grew each year.

Facing the ache of unfulfilled longings is a challenge for everyone, not only singles. Perhaps you long for the salvation of a loved one, physical or emotional healing for yourself or a child, reconciliation with an estranged family member, a flourishing career that "fits," a soul mate in a friend or spouse, or new life in a dry marriage.

As we walk on our journey of faith, how do we cope with unfulfilled longings? How do we embrace life—living it fully, joyfully, and passionately with faith, hope, and trust—even when our hearts ache with unmet desires? The more I have experienced and observed this struggle, the more I have wondered about it.

I wondered when I received a call from a friend 2,000 miles away who sobbed on the phone, "He doesn't love me!" After relaying her conversation with the man she'd been dating—and in love with—for the past year, she wept, "I'm thirty-three years old. How long am I going to have to wait for someone who will love me?"

I wondered when another friend came over in tears about the difficulties in her marriage. "It wasn't supposed to be like this." She went on to describe the type of relationship she'd expected and longed for.

I wondered as I ached with a dear friend whose son was born with three holes in his heart. Though she's been praying for his healing since his birth five years ago, he's about to undergo another open-heart surgery.

All of us face the reality of unmet desires. And, like those who suffer physical disabilities, we may have to live with certain longings unfulfilled for a lifetime. Yet as we embrace this mystery, we find our longings can lead us to something even better than their fulfillment.

NO GUARANTEES

When I was in college, I heard Psalm 37:4 quoted almost as an unconditional certainty that God would fulfill our desires (particularly for a spouse): "Delight yourself in the Lord; and He will give you the desires of your heart." Yet as I read the whole of Scripture, I see a gracious God who often does grant our yearnings but offers no guarantee that He always will. Our desire for marriage, family, healing, and many other legitimate needs are not unscriptural, and God very often grants them— but not always. He never promised to give us everything we wanted. Instead, He promised to give us everything we need, and we are to trust Him with the rest.

Every good and perfect gift comes from Him, not because we deserve it, but because He is gracious (James 1:17). Thank God, He has not given us what we deserve, but everything we don't: love, grace, compassion. . . . And thankfully He gives us what is good. But our definition of what is good for us may radically differ from His.

Several years ago, after meeting a man to whom I felt attracted, I desired a relationship between us. When it didn't happen, I began moaning to God about how He seemed to be depriving me—not only of that relationship but of any relationship with a man. And what was God's response? *"I am not depriving you. I am sparing you."*

Now I look back with utter relief and thanksgiving that He spared me from unnecessary pain. "God does not just give me what I want," my pastor reminded me one Sunday. "He gives me everything I would want if I knew everything He knows."

God wants us to be real with Him about our longings—to honestly tell Him about them rather than deny or dismiss them. He also wants to protect us from worshiping our desires. A friend of mine wanted to go to the mission field, but was waiting until God granted her request for a husband. She said, "Why should I serve overseas when He hasn't given me what I've asked for?"

When we elevate the fulfillment of our desires above faithfulness to God, we are handing over the keys of our heart to an intoxicated driver. We allow our passions, not God, to steer us. John Calvin observed: "The evil in our desires typically does not lie in what we want, but that we want it *too much*." When we allow our yearnings to control us, we create and worship an idol.

How do we live with longings without allowing them to overcome us? The answer lies not in dismissing them as unspiritual or unimportant, but in embracing them as part of our humanness—and, more importantly, directing their fire to fuel our passion for Christ.

THE BLESSING OF LONGINGS

A friend e-mailed me about his struggle with the breakup of a relationship: "I was praying the other night and told the Lord, 'I don't want to love someone and they not love me back.' The

Lord spoke to me, and said, *'I know what you mean.'* "

Unfulfilled longings can be a blessing from God as they teach us about His heart. God feels our struggles more than we can imagine. The Old Testament prophets portray how He longs with grief for His wayward children: "My heart is turned over within Me" (Hosea 11:8).

As we wait with longing for the fulfillment of our hearts' desires, He waits with longing for the fulfillment of His desire: that no man should perish but all should return to their Creator (2 Peter 3:9). In our pain, we better understand God's heart.

Jesus describes the yearning of the prodigal son's father, who daily waits and watches for the young man's return. After years of longing, he finally glimpses his rag-covered son entering the gate. As the father runs out to embrace him—his heart's desire— we also glimpse God's longing and ache for the coming home of His beloved children.

Not only does God long for the return of those who have wandered from Him, He also longs for us who follow Him to enjoy simply sitting with Him. A. W. Tozer noted, "He waits to be wanted. Too bad that with many of us he waits so long, so very long, in vain."[1]

Longings can often feel like a curse. Yet perhaps they mysteriously are God-given gifts in our lives. Like Paul's unanswered prayers for healing, they keep us dependent upon our Sustainer (2 Corinthians 12:9–10). If one day God fulfills our longing in this life, we will less likely depend upon it to sustain us, for we've already experienced His grace, which alone is sufficient.

Longings also bless us as they increase our hunger for heaven. They point us to what God offers, which this world promises but fails to deliver. Unfulfilled desires turn our eyes to our real home where untainted joy awaits us, joy that will never wither from loss, lack, or wear. They remind us that Paradise— heaven—is the only place we will experience ultimate fulfillment. When we set our desires toward things on earth rather than the glorious things of God's kingdom, we set our appetites too low.

In the thirteenth century Thomas à Kempis wrote words that still ring true today: "You cannot be satisfied with any temporal good, because you were not created to enjoy these alone. If you desire inordinately the things that are present, you shall lose those which are heavenly and eternal."[2]

OUR REAL DESIRE

As we embrace our longings, we more clearly recognize the root of our desires. And only by recognizing the root can we ever find true fulfillment. St. Augustine—describing the pursuit in his youth to find satisfaction in women, debate, excitement, food, and possessions—unearths his true passions: "The single desire that documented my search for delight was simply *to love and be loved*."[3]

Underneath our deepest desires is the aching to be wholly loved in a way that only God can love us. My longing for a spouse is really a longing to be fully known and fully loved, for one to see and know all about me and still be totally committed to me despite all my foibles and flaws. In truth, only Christ can *wholly* meet that desire. Only Christ's love will never disappoint. "How great is the love the Father has lavished on us" (1 John 3:1 NIV). We are already as deeply loved as we could ever hope to be.

In *Desiring God*, John Piper discusses our deepest longings:

> Saving faith is the confidence that if you forsake all sinful pleasures, the hidden treasure of holy joy will satisfy your deepest desires. Saving faith is the heartfelt conviction not only that Christ is reliable, but also that he is desirable. It is the confidence that he will come through with his promises and that what he promises is more to be desired than all the world.[4]

When we recognize the root of our longings, they lose the

power we may be tempted to give them. Rather than the meat of our lives, they become the appetizer to prepare our stomachs for the *real* meal. Jesus said to His followers, "I am the bread of life. He who comes to me will never go hungry" (John 6:35 NIV).

When I lived in Asia, my first Chinese banquet mystified me. As the waiters carried enticing and flavorful-smelling dishes—stuffed peppers, shrimp pot stickers, pinecone fish—to our table, Desirée and I dug in. However, our Chinese colleagues had only a few bites. We assumed they held back in traditional fashion so *we* could enjoy more. Yet over the course of the next two hours, the dishes kept coming.

Well into the banquet, a waiter brought a huge platter of the most glistening and ornately decorated chicken I'd ever seen. Our host excitedly exclaimed, "This the gold medal!" as he loaded our bowls with succulent meat. But by the time the prized dish had come, Desirée and I could hardly open our mouths for another bite. Only then did we realize the first rounds of dishes were merely appetizers.

When we stuff ourselves on appetizers in life, we save no room for the true meal. Appetizers were never intended to *satiate* our appetite, but to *stimulate* our appetite for the main course. Appetizers *are* good and tasty. And fulfilled desires, like appetizers, do satisfy some of our needs. But we must never mistake them for the meat that nourishes our souls. Hear God's wisdom for us: "Why do you spend money for what is not bread, and your wages for what does not satisfy? Listen carefully to Me, and eat what is good, and delight yourself in abundance" (Isaiah 55:2).

When stuffed on appetizers, we leave little room for the gold medal—Jesus. We walk away bloated but unsatisfied. Only the Living Bread satisfies the deepest hunger of our hearts. Only the Living Water can truly quench our thirst (John 6:35).

In C. S. Lewis's *The Silver Chair*, Jill encounters the great and terrifying Lion and King, Aslan, as she walks panting toward a stream:

"Are you not thirsty?" said the Lion.

"I'm dying of thirst," said Jill.

"Then drink," said the Lion.

"May I—could I—would you mind going away while I do?" said Jill.

The Lion answered this only by a look and a very low growl. And as Jill gazed at its motionless bulk, she realized that she might as well have asked the whole mountain to move aside for her convenience.

The delicious rippling noise of the stream was driving her nearly frantic.

"Will you promise not to—do anything to me, if I do come?" said Jill.

Jill was so thirsty now that, without noticing it, she had come a step nearer.

"Do you eat girls?" she said.

"I have swallowed up girls and boys, women and men, kings and emperors, cities and realms," said the Lion. It didn't just say this as if it were boasting, nor as if it were sorry, nor as if it were angry. It just said it.

"I daren't come and drink," said Jill.

"Then you will die of thirst," said the Lion.

"Oh, dear!" said Jill, coming another step nearer. "I suppose I must go and look for another stream then."

"There is no other stream," said the Lion.[5]

There is no other stream—no other stream but God. More than filling our longings, God wants to give us *himself.*

FUEL FOR PASSION

Unfulfilled longings can also be mysterious blessings in that they can fuel our passion for Christ. We can ask God to channel the passion we feel for certain things we'd like to have or experience into a passion and longing for Him.

The word *desire* in certain places of Scripture has also been translated "delight." When we delight in something, we also desire it. When we delight ourselves in God, He becomes our most compelling desire. Rather than reading Psalm 37:4—"Delight yourself in the Lord; and He will give you the desires of your heart"—as a guarantee that God will give us what we want, we recognize that our heart's deepest desires were written for Him. A. W. Tozer noted, "God is so vastly wonderful, so utterly and completely delightful that He can, without anything other than Himself, meet and overflow the deepest demands of our total nature, mysterious and deep as that nature is."[6]

Our deepest desire *is* fulfilled as we delight ourselves in Him—because He fills it with *himself*. No longer do our desires compel us; our thirst for God does.

Asaph writes, "Being with you, I desire nothing on earth" (Psalm 73:25 NIV). Time alone with God quiets the intensity of our longings—just as time away from Him churns them. When I've neglected time in quiet with God—being filled by Him—my desire for affection, love, and affirmation from others intensifies. I realized this one morning when I awoke and, ignoring my practice of sitting down to spend time with God, headed straight for my computer. I was more eager to hear, "You've got mail," than to hear the voice of God through Scripture. Brennan Manning observes, "The indispensable condition for developing and maintaining the awareness of our belovedness is time alone with God."[7] When we do not take occasion to be alone, we lack the awareness of our belovedness and begin yearning for a sense of it through other people or activities.

God says, "Open your mouth wide and I will fill it" (Psalm 81:10). As we spend time with Him, He satisfies our soul's deepest desire. "Because Your love is better than life . . . my soul will be satisfied as with the richest of foods" (Psalm 63:3, 5 NIV).

BETWEEN THE NOW AND THE NOT YET

Does this mean our longings for things other than God are inconsequential? No. We *do* feel the pain of unmet desires. We *will* have tough times. Some days seem harder than others as we face another negative pregnancy test, another bounced check, another night returning to an empty apartment, another doctor's waiting room, another argument with our spouse, or whatever it may be.

God's heart grieves with us over our unfulfilled longings. When Jesus came to Mary and Martha and saw their pain after their brother Lazarus had died, He was deeply moved in spirit and troubled (John 11:34–35). Even knowing what He was about to do, He wept with them in their grief, as I believe He weeps with us in ours.

On those days when our desires become too strong to bear, when the intensity of longing overwhelms us, we can come to God. Just as He daily bears our burden (Psalm 68:19), we can ask Him to carry our desires when they are too heavy for us. We can rest knowing they are safely in His hands and that He will gently take care of them. Not that He will necessarily grant our requests, but He will hold them for you with great tenderness. He cares about the cares of our hearts (1 Peter 5:7). We do have hope, not that He will fulfill all our desires, but that He, our Redeemer, can redeem for His glory even the strongest yearnings in our lives.

Corrie ten Boom, a former prisoner in a Nazi concentration camp, writes,

> Does God answer our prayers? Often, but not always. Why? Because He knows what we don't know. He knows everything.
>
> When we get to heaven, we'll thank God for all the answered prayers. But it may be that we will thank Him for the unanswered prayers even more, because then we will be able to see things from God's perspective. We will see that God never makes mistakes.[8]

As I read Hebrews 11 one day, I wondered, *Why, God?* My eyes followed down the long list of saints who gave their lives for God, left everything behind, obeyed Him wholly—yet still did not all obtain His promises. Some did—escaping swords, conquering kingdoms, quenching fiery furnaces. Others did not—they were stoned, sawed in two, pierced with blades (Hebrews 11:33–40).

I find it interesting that the writer of Hebrews would include those who did *not* obtain the promises. Why would God choose to grant some the promises in this life, while some had to wait until the next? Why would He not save those being sawed in two—or those of us who feel our hearts are being torn in half? And why would some of our longings remain unfulfilled even when we are faithful to what He calls us to do? Perhaps the list serves to remind us that unanswered prayers and longings are not a sign of our—or God's—unfaithfulness. Perhaps they are mysteries we will not understand this side of eternity.

As with some of the saints in Hebrews 11, we may never see certain promises or dreams fulfilled while on Earth. Yet as we live between the now and the not yet, we have great hope knowing that our deepest longing—the desire underneath all our human passions—is fulfilled in Christ's love for us.

Listen again to Asaph's exclamation: "Whom have I in heaven but Thee? And besides Thee, I desire nothing on earth. My flesh and my heart may fail, but God is the strength of my heart and my portion forever" (Psalm 73:25–26). The key to living with unfulfilled longings lies not in denying or cursing our desires, or trying to fill our desires on our own, but in desiring God more than anything else.

One evening after discussing marriage with the man I loved, we held each other quietly while worship music played on my stereo. As the refrain of the song played—"Nothing is as lovely, nothing is as worthy, nothing is a wonderful as knowing You"—tears trickled down my face. It dawned on me that here sat next to me this amazing man whom I deeply loved, to whom I could soon be married, yet it wasn't enough. A potential husband, no matter how wonderful, was not enough to meet my deepest desire. No man could satisfy me like I longed to be satisfied because no man was intended to completely fulfill me. In that moment I realized emotionally what I'd always known cognitively: Only Jesus is sufficient to meet my deepest longing.

My pastor, Reverend Fred Harrell, often reminds our congregation that though he has a gorgeous wife and four darling children whom he adores, "It's not enough. *It was never meant to be.*"

We can embrace our unfulfilled longings as mysterious blessings when we allow them to lead us to the only One who *is* enough.

THE MYSTERY OF DESIRE: REFLECTIONS

QUESTIONS FOR JOURNAL AND/OR SMALL GROUP

1. What does a longing in your life teach you about God?
2. What appetizers have you been tempted to feast upon to satisfy you that have distracted your passion for Christ?
3. Ask God to speak to you about your longing as you sit in silence before Him.
4. Picture your longing as a backpack that has been weighing you down as you've carried it around. Imagine removing the straps from your shoulders, handing the whole thing to God, and letting Him carry it for you.

VERSES TO TREASURE

If any man is thirsty, let him come to Me and drink. He who believes in Me, as the Scripture said, "From his innermost being shall flow rivers of living water" (John 7:37–38).

Ho! Every one who thirsts, come to the waters; and you who have no money come, buy and eat. Come, buy wine and milk without money and without cost. . . . Listen carefully to Me, and eat what is good, and delight yourself in abundance. (Isaiah 55:1–2)

Blessed are those who hunger and thirst for righteousness, for they shall be satisfied. (Matthew 5:6)

All my springs of joy are in You. (Psalm 87:7)

"The Lord is my portion," says my soul. (Lamentations 3:24)

How blessed are all those who long for Him. (Isaiah 30:18)

THOUGHTS FOR CONTEMPLATION

"For I tell you this, one loving, blind *desire for God alone* is more valuable in itself, more pleasing to God and to the saints, more beneficial to your own growth, and more helpful to your friends, both living and dead, than anything else you could do."
—*The Cloud of Unknowing*

"What about when . . . the prayer goes unanswered? Just keep praying . . . keep on beating a path to God's door, because one thing you can be sure of is that down the path you beat with even your halting prayer, the God you call upon will finally come, and even if he does not bring you the answer you want, he will bring you himself. And maybe at the secret heart of all our prayers that is what we are really praying for."
—Frederick Buechner, *Wishful Thinking: A Theological ABC*

"God Himself is the portion of the saints."

—John Bunyan

"Man's highest happiness consists in holiness, for it is by this that the reasonable creature is united to God, the fountain of all good. Happiness doth so essentially consist in knowing, loving, and serving God. . . . No other enjoyments or privileges will make a man happy without this."

—Jonathan Edwards, Charity and Its Fruits

"Again and again Jesus said: 'It is I; it is I. It is I that am highest; it is I that you love; it is I you enjoy; it is I that you serve. It is I that you long for; it is I that you desire. It is I that am all.' "

—Julian of Norwich

"When the Lord divided Canaan among the tribes of Israel, Levi received no share of the land. God said to him simply, 'I am thy part and thy inheritance,' and by those words made him richer than all his brethren, richer than all the kings and rajahs who have ever lived in the world. And there is a spiritual principle here, a principle still valid for every priest of the Most High God. The man who has God for his treasure has all things in One. Many ordinary treasures [marriage, children, success, beauty, strength] may be denied him, or if he is allowed to have them, the enjoyment of them will be so tempered that they will never be necessary to his happiness. Or if he must see them go, one after one, he will scarcely feel a sense of loss, for having the Source of all things he has in One all satisfaction, all pleasure, all delight."

—A. W. Tozer, The Pursuit of God

HYMN: "Jesus, Thou Joy of Loving Hearts"

Jesus, Thou Joy of loving hearts,
Thou fount of life, Thou light of men,
From the best bliss that earth imparts,
We turn unfilled to Thee again.

We taste thee, O Thou living Bread,
And long to feast upon Thee still;
We drink of Thee, the Fountainhead,
And thirst our souls from Thee to fill.

Our restless spirits yearn for Thee,

Where'er our changeful lot is cast:
Glad when Thy gracious smile we see,
Blest when our faith can hold Thee fast.

O Jesus, ever with us stay;
Make all our moments calm and bright;
Chase the dark night of sin away;
Shed o'er the world Thy holy light.

PRAYER

Lord, I long so deeply for _____. *I commit this desire and myself to you because I do not know what to do about it. May I lay this longing as an offering before you—trusting in your goodness, believing in your sovereignty, resting in your love. Use this desire as a mysterious blessing in my life to teach me more about your heart. Help me remember that only you are the one who can fully satisfy my desires.*

O Lord, stir the flames of holy desire in my heart and give me a passionate longing after you.

8

SEEING THE UNSEEN:

THE MYSTERY OF HOPE

As long as matters are really hopeful, hope is mere flattery or platitude. It is only when everything is hopeless that hope begins to be a strength at all. Like all the Christian virtues, it is as unreasonable as it is indispensable.

G. K. Chesterton

This hope we have as an anchor of the soul, a hope both sure and steadfast.

Hebrews 6:19

YOU CAN ALWAYS SPOT a tourist at the San Francisco airport in summertime. Dressed for sunshine in shorts and a summer top, they shiver while waiting for a shuttle to rescue them from the chilly blanket of fog enveloping the city. If the fog persists throughout their visit, they'll have a hard time believing that a sparkling blue ocean lies beyond the towering red peaks of the Golden Gate Bridge, that the stately Transamerica building spirals high into the sky, or that breathtaking views stretch across the bay. The heavy mist hides them all. When day after day dense wet gray dampens the streets, even locals, bundled up in long pants and jackets, begin to wonder if the sun really does exist.

During my most difficult times, when a sense of hopelessness like thick fog enveloped me, I began to wonder if rays of light would ever again shine in my life. I threw my hands down in frustration, exclaiming to myself and to God: "I am just not going to hope anymore because my dreams are constantly being broken!"

All of us have days—sometimes seasons—when despair hovers. Though the knowledge of hope in Christ may fill the reservoirs of our minds, our hearts pant with thirst for hope for today. How do we draw from those reservoirs during the barren times in our lives? How do we hope when we know we *will* face future disappointments—whether it be recurring illness, a special-needs child, financial burdens, or any number of difficult situations?

How do we embrace hope when nothing in our earthly future looks promising? Margaret, one of the most bubbly and positive people I've known, wrote me several years ago while grieving the end of her relationship with the man she thought she would marry. A year after he pulled away, she still battled hopelessness. "I am not really sure what brings on the tears," she shared. "It's not a sadness that makes me unable to function—it's just kind of dull, aching despair and the recognition that I don't really look forward to anything in this life. I am thankful every day for opportunities to encourage and serve others, and to praise God, but I don't really *hope* for anything."

I've also experienced that feeling. When illness eclipsed my dream of working overseas again, my future stretched before me like a dark narrow path winding through mist-covered woods. Around that time I visited a friend. In contrast to mine, her future dazzled bright like a wide golden road before her—an overseas career in an international company with seemingly endless potential. She was living my dream, while I was living what at times felt more like a nightmare.

As we gathered in her home for a prayer meeting one evening, the leader (who knew nothing about me) said he sensed someone was dealing with hopelessness. *That would be me.* Though outwardly cheerful, inwardly I cringed every time this dark cloud threatened to descend upon me—washing away the tiniest seed of expectation I had. No matter how hard I had prayed, I couldn't make my way out from under it. I revealed my feelings to the group.

That night, as they gathered around to pray for me, one woman exhorted me to reject the spirit of hopelessness and claim the promise of God that there is hope for the future and "your hope will not be cut off" (Proverbs 23:18). I was so tired of hoping, claiming, believing, and then being disappointed again. But as they began to pray and claim God's promises—promises that when I spoke them felt like empty words—something changed. Nothing felt different that night, but slowly, ever so slowly, the cloud began to lift. A tiny seed of expectancy began to sprout.

A DIFFERENT KIND OF HOPE

When the crowd crammed into the house in Capernaum to hear Jesus, "there was no longer room, even near the door" (Mark 2:2), but that did not stop the friends of the paralytic. They knew that an encounter with Jesus would forever change him, though they did not know for certain just how. They removed the roof tiles, made a sufficient opening, and lowered him on his pallet into the home. Jesus, seeing their faith, said to the man, "Your sins are forgiven. . . . Rise, take up your pallet and go home" (Mark 2:5, 11). Though he had presumably lost all hope of ever walking—how often are paralytics healed?—his friends carried hope for him as they carried him to Jesus.

Like those friends of the paralytic, and those of mine in the prayer group, my sister, Sheri, held hope for me. When I voiced my fears about my future—whether or not I would ever meet someone to love and be loved by, whether I could pursue dreams, whether healing would come—she often assured with great conviction, "Stacey, I really have hope for your future. I really sense good things are up ahead." Though I could not see the sun, I glimpsed it through her eyes. She carried hope for me when I was unable to rise up from my pallet of despondency and walk.

When the two disciples walked the road to Emmaus after Jesus' death, the man walking beside them, unbeknown to them, was the risen Lord. As they explained to Him the events of Jesus' death (of which He appeared ignorant), they sighed, "We were *hoping* that it was He who was going to redeem Israel" (Luke 24:21, emphasis added).

They were anticipating redemption—*political and temporal.* Yet fulfillment of this looked nothing like they'd expected. The devastating events of Jesus' crucifixion extinguished all their hope that Jesus would become King of Israel. But these events that they interpreted as dashing all hopes were the very events to bring about more redemption than they had ever longed for—*spiritual and eternal*. Seven miles they had walked with Jesus, lamenting their dashed hopes, while all the way Hope was walking right beside them. "In the moment in which we feel abandoned by both our dreams and the God we thought would save them for us," writes Craig Barnes, "in precisely that moment we are ready to receive God's true salvation. It is then we discover that God wants to save us, not our dreams."[1]

After facing unanswered questions, disappointments, losses, pains, and broken dreams, we want to pull our hearts and souls inward, like a hermit crab retreating into his shell. We guard ourselves even against God's promises so that we might not be hurt again, disappointed again, or broken again. But perhaps those very events that seem to slay our dreams are the means to bring about the *deeper* things for which we hope. The disciples had yet to understand the greater thing God was doing through Christ's death. We also may have yet to understand the greater things God is doing in our life and the lives of those around us through dashed hopes.

HOPE OF REDEMPTION

After enduring betrayal by his own family, slavery in a foreign land, and years of imprisonment, Joseph still could say to his brothers: "You meant evil against me, but God *meant* it for good in order to bring about this present result, to preserve many people alive" (Genesis 50:20, emphasis added). God did not place Joseph in his position to save Israel *in spite of* the hardships and events that seemed to crush all of Joseph's hope. He placed Joseph there *through* them.

God meant it for good. He *intended* it all along—even in the loneliness of the dungeon, the darkness of the pit, the sting of betrayal, the bite of false accusations—for good! Through the very events God appeared to overlook, He not only saved, protected, and exalted Joseph, but He also used the evil against him in order to save many others. That which appeared to crush all of Joseph's hopes actually brought about hope to a famine-starved nation. Hope assures us that God can redeem all things, even evil, for good in our lives and the lives of others.

Job, with his skin clinging to his bones, boils covering his body, tears of grief pouring from his eyes, had every reason, like Joseph, to give up all hope:

> God . . . has closed His net around me. . . . He has walled up my way so that I cannot pass; and He has put darkness on my paths. He has stripped my honor from me. . . . He breaks me down on every side, and I am gone; and *He has uprooted my hope like a tree.* . . . My relatives have failed me, and my intimate friends have forgotten me . . . and those I love have turned against me. (Job 19:6, 8–10, 14, 17, 19, emphasis added)

Yet even in all his pain, something enabled Job to turn the corner from despair toward hope. What was it? It was knowing that God is a God of redemption. "And as for me, I know that my *Redeemer* lives, and at the last He will take His stand on the earth" (Job 19:25). In grief and agony, Job remembered the end of the story: *redemption.* Though he had no guarantee he'd see it while on Earth, he claimed, "Even after my skin is destroyed, yet from my flesh I shall see God" (v. 26).

HOPING AGAIN AFTER DISAPPOINTMENT

What about when disappointment comes—when dreams have been broken? As I became stronger physically, and more hopeful emotionally, I began to dream again for the first time in a long while.

God seemed to clearly open the door for an opportunity to lead a college student program to China, similar to one I'd had to turn down several times over the past five years. I now finally felt strong enough to lead. After six months of preparation for the semester program—with orientation completed, funds

THE MYSTERY OF HOPE / 143

raised, immunizations taken, visa stamped, tickets purchased, and bags packed—I was ready to get on the plane. Three days before our departure my body relapsed with a virus that kept me in bed. I rescheduled my flight for a few days later, certain I would recuperate. My co-leader took the team without me, and we planned to meet in Beijing. As week after week passed and the virus continued to rage within me, my dream once again crumbled.

Jeremiah, facing the ache of disappointment, wrote,

> My soul has been rejected from peace; I have forgotten happiness. So I say, "My strength has perished, and so has my hope from the Lord." Remember my affliction and my wandering, the wormwood and bitterness. Surely my soul remembers and is bowed down within me. (Lamentations 3:17–20)

Like many of God's followers throughout Scripture, Jeremiah in no way minimizes the anguish his soul has tasted. But with the next breath he declares,

> This I recall to mind, therefore I have hope. The Lord's lovingkindnesses indeed never cease, for His compassions never fail. They are new every morning; great is Thy faithfulness. "The Lord is my portion," says my soul, "therefore I have hope in Him" (Lamentations 3:21–24).

Even we who have tasted weakness, wandering, and bitterness can embrace hope! Our hope, like Jeremiah's, can flourish when we place it in God and His steadfast character, for it lies not in something but in Someone. Like Job who lost everything, we can say in times of disappointment, "Though He slay me, I will hope in Him" (13:15).

As God has been stabilizing and strengthening my health, I have begun dreaming again. But I know that I will face future disappointments. I know that dreams still will be broken, and to be honest, that scares me. I don't want to go through this disillusionment again. I don't want to hope again for love only to end up broken again. I don't want to pursue a dream and fail because my body or other limitations prevent me from achieving what my spirit can envision.

Yet ultimately our hope lies not in our dreams—or in our strength, abilities, loved ones, career, or in us. In fact, broken dreams and loss of hope unearths what, apart from God, we have placed our hope upon. A sense of hopelessness can free us to build our hope, in the words of the hymn, "on nothing less than Jesus' blood and righteousness." For only when wholly set upon Christ does hope not disappoint (Romans 5:5).

When Christ walked with the disciples on the road to Emmaus after His resurrection, He said, "O foolish men and slow of heart to believe! . . . Was it not necessary for the Christ to suffer these things and to enter into His glory?" (Luke 24:25–26). But the disciples still didn't get it. They still clung to *their* picture of hope, preventing their eyes from recognizing Him. Only when Christ broke the bread—His body, in which they had placed their hope—did their eyes open. "And breaking it, he began giving it to them. And their eyes were opened and they recognized him" (vv. 30–31). Only when their hope in His earthly body (and their image of an earthly king of Israel) was broken did their eyes open to true Hope. Perhaps God sometimes allows our earthly hopes to be broken in order that our hope may rest more fully upon Him.

Though waves of trials may crash over us, they cannot shipwreck us or take away the living Hope within us. The apostle Paul, who daily faced threats of death, stated, "We are afflicted in every way, but not crushed; perplexed, but not despairing; persecuted, but not forsaken; struck down, but not destroyed" (2 Corinthians 4:8–9).

Though dreams can be taken away, hope *cannot* be taken away—only relinquished. When we relinquish hope, we not only lose our ability to risk and dream, we also close the door for God to work wonders in the midst of our disappointment. When we take a risk, we take a step of hope, even when we feel we have none. We demonstrate the hope that good things can come, even though no sign exists now.

When the Babylonians besieged Jerusalem, the prophet Jeremiah demonstrated the risk of hope by following God's direction to buy a field at Anathoth. The witnesses to his purchase no doubt snickered in skepticism: "The Babylonians already captured Anathoth. The property is worthless! Only a fool would make such a purchase!" Yet God directed Jeremiah to buy it as a sign of future restoration for the exiles, telling them, "Houses and fields and vineyards shall again be bought in this land" (Jeremiah 32:15).

FUELING OUR HOPE

During a time of brokenheartedness, I awoke some mornings feeling like a Mack truck had parked on my chest. Any hopefulness for joy and good that day sunk under the weight of pain. Yet by God's grace, I reminded myself, "This too shall pass. No matter how my heart grieves over the loss of this relationship, this too shall pass. The Lord is good in all He does. All shall be well."

I was not simply practicing the power of positive thinking; I was *confessing* what is true and letting the belt of truth and the shield of faith (Ephesians 6:14–16) strengthen me when I was losing balance. Rather than listen to the lie that my future had no hope and that God was forgetting me, meditating on the truth opened channels from the reservoir of hope in my head to fill my fainting heart.

As my pastor often says, when the coals of hope smolder, we can fuel it by "preaching to ourselves." We can remind ourselves daily or hourly, however and whenever needed, that God is the Source of our hope. Jeremiah practiced preaching to himself when he said, "This I recall to mind, therefore I have hope." He then proceeded to recount the character of the One who held his life in His hands: loving, kind, compassionate, faithful (Lamentations 3:21). God's Word has supernatural power to fuel our hope.

Ten months after that prayer meeting at my friend's in which the clouds of hopelessness slowly started to lift, I stumbled upon another anchor from Jeremiah:

> I have loved you with an everlasting love; therefore I have drawn you with lovingkindness. Again I will rebuild you, and you shall be rebuilt, O virgin of Israel. You shall take up your tambourines, and go forth to the dances of the merrymakers . . . and [you] shall come and shout for joy . . . and there is hope for your future. (31:3–4, 12, 17)

No longer feeling hopeless, but not feeling particularly hopeful, how desperately I wanted to claim that passage as a promise for my future. Yet if I did, wouldn't I only be setting myself up for greater disappointment? As I kept coming across the same passage at unexpected times, I suspected God wanted me to believe this by faith even when it seemed furthest from reality. Being rebuilt? Taking up a tambourine with shouts of joy? Dancing with merrymakers? Hope for my future? Whether it was intended to be a promise for this life or the next, I decided to claim it. A twinge of reluctant hope sprouted.

A year later and a little more hopeful, as I strolled a street fair with friends, I spotted a tambourine for sale. Something prompted me to buy it and keep it as a reminder of that promise—that someday I will shake a tambourine with shouts of joy and dancing. Sometimes, when tempted to feel hopeless, I even shake it now, in hope and faith of what God will do.

Whether we feel hopeful or not, hope is not something we muster up. Though we can strengthen our hope by choosing continually to set our hope upon God and by reading His Word, ultimately hope is a gift from God. A gift, in the words of Julian of Norwich, that "spills down to us by the grace of God."[2] When we feel hopeless, rather than try to conjure up false feelings, we can pray, and ask others to pray, that God would grant us the gift of hope. Paul prays this way for the Romans: "Now may the God of hope fill you with all joy and peace in believing, that you may abound in hope by the power of the Holy Spirit" (15:13). We can pray the same for ourselves and for others.

GOD OF THE RESURRECTION

For lo, the winter is past, the rain is over and gone. The flowers appear on the earth; the time of singing has come. (Song of Solomon 2:11–12)

Sometimes the winter can feel so long, as if it will never end. Yet God reminds us every year in His creation that no matter how long and cold winter may feel, spring *will* come again. No matter how naked and dead the trees appear in January, green shoots will sprout. No matter how hidden lie the roots of flowers, magenta tulips and grape hyacinth will surge and shout new life. New vitality *will* come again. As God promises Jeremiah during the siege of Jerusalem, "Fields shall be bought in this land of which you say, 'It is a desolation. . . . ' For I will restore their fortunes" (32:43–44).

My friend Margaret, whose letter I quoted early in this chapter, just called me last week. She and her husband, David, the man whom she had grieved over for almost two years, just celebrated the birth of their second child. No matter what our story, we do know the ending—whether on this earth or in the world to come: We will all be shaking tambourines. For "God has planned for us . . . a praising glorious life" to come (Ephesians 1:14 THE MESSAGE).

Though we rejoice when we experience fulfilled longings, healed bodies, and mended hearts in this lifetime, ultimately these are not our source of hope. Hope comes not through realized dreams or even answered prayers. Hope comes through Christ in us, the Hope of glory (Colossians 1:27).

We need not wait until eternity to begin experiencing the hope we have. For, as the apostle Peter wrote,

> Because Jesus was raised from the dead, we've been given a brand new life and have everything to live for, including a future in heaven—*and the future starts now.* God is keeping careful watch over us and the future. The day is coming when you'll have it all, life healed and whole. (1 Peter 1:3–6 THE MESSAGE, emphasis added)

What a promise! We may have days and seasons when our future looks bleak, when being healed and whole seems an eternity away. But in the mystery of hope, we can *now* begin to experience the joy of eternal life as we grow in intimacy with Jesus. For "this is eternal life, that they may *know* Me" (John 17:3, emphasis added).

"The Word made flesh for us," said Hildegard of Bingen in the twelfth century, "gives us the greatest hope that the murky night of darkness will not overwhelm us, but we shall see the daylight of eternity." God grants us no promise that we will avoid any of the tragedies of this life, but He does promise redemption and, ultimately, resurrection. Facing difficulties, for some the journey without hope may feel like the seven-mile road to Emmaus. For others it may seem like a seventy-mile road. But no matter how long our road, *Hope* walks beside us.

I always love flying out of the San Francisco airport during the summer, because as the plane ascends through the fog, suddenly sunshine splashes into the windows! I want to shout, "It's there! It was there all along! Just as bright; just as powerful; just as strong as I had remembered—even more so." The thick, wet fog of hopelessness, no matter how long it seems to hover, is temporal. Hope—Christ—is eternal.

THE MYSTERY OF HOPE: REFLECTIONS

QUESTIONS FOR JOURNAL AND/OR SMALL GROUP

1. Where is a place in your life that you feel hopeless?
2. Have dashed hopes unearthed what you have placed your hope in apart from Christ?
3. Is there someone you could ask to pray with you for hope?
4. If your hopes are faltering, how can you encourage yourself as Jeremiah did?

VERSES TO TREASURE/PROMISES TO CLAIM

My soul, wait in silence for God only, for my hope is from Him. (Psalm 62:5)

Set your hope fully on the grace to be given you when Jesus Christ is revealed. (1 Peter 1:13 NIV)

Why are you in despair, O my soul? And why have you become disturbed within me? Hope in God, for I shall again praise Him for the help of His presence. (Psalm 42:5)

I wait for the Lord, my soul does wait, and in His word do I hope. (Psalm 130:5)

Hope does not disappoint, because the love of God has been poured out within our hearts through the Holy Spirit who was given to us. (Romans 5:5)

Now may the God of hope fill you with all joy and peace in believing that you may abound in hope by the power of the Holy Spirit. (Romans 15:13)

THOUGHTS TO CONTEMPLATE

"Hope arises out of the hard truth of how things are. Christians will always live carrying in one hand the promises of how it will be and in the other the hard reality of how it is. To deny either is to hold only half the truth of the gospel."

—Craig Barnes, *Yearning*

"The good news of the gospel is that we don't have to live without hope. Despair turns to hope on the cross."

—Bob Blackford, *Heaven's Back Row*

HYMN: "The Solid Rock"

My hope is built on nothing less
Than Jesus' blood and righteousness.
I dare not trust the sweetest frame,
But wholly lean on Jesus' name.
On Christ, the solid Rock, I stand—
All other ground is sinking sand;
All other ground is sinking sand.

When darkness veils his lovely face,
I rest on his unchanging grace;
In ev'ry high and stormy gale
My anchor holds within the veil.
On Christ, the solid Rock, I stand—
All other ground is sinking sand;
All other ground is sinking sand.

His oath, his covenant, his blood
Support me in the whelming flood;
When all around my soul gives way,
He then is all my hope and stay.
On Christ, the solid Rock, I stand—
All other ground is sinking sand;
All other ground is sinking sand.

When he shall come with trumpet sound,
O may I then in him be found,
Dressed in His righteousness alone,
Faultless to stand before the throne.
On Christ, the solid Rock, I stand—
All other ground is sinking sand;
All other ground is sinking sand.

PRAYER

"O Lord, my God, give me again the courage to hope. Merciful God, let hope again make fertile my sterile and barren mind."

—Søren Kierkegaard

9

CELEBRATING OUR BELOVEDNESS:

THE MYSTERY OF GOD'S DELIGHT

It will no longer be said to you, "Forsaken," . . . but you will be called, "My delight is in her" . . . for the Lord delights in you. . . . As the bridegroom rejoices over the bride, so your God will rejoice over you.

Isaiah 62:4–5

He will take great delight in you.

Zephaniah 3:17 NIV

I OPENED THE BRIGHTLY colored bon voyage card and read my sister's words: "As you embark on this new adventure, let God love you. . . ."

Let God love me? Something in her words made me catch my breath. *What does she mean? Of course I let God love me,* I thought a bit defensively. *How couldn't I?* However, I suspected she saw something that I feared to admit. Could it be true— could it be I *don't* let God love me? Could it be, perhaps, God loves me so much more than I experience because I resist His love, resist His goodness toward me?

Cognitively, I knew He loved me, for Scripture clearly states, "God so loved the world." (I could quote John 3:16 without a thought.) Yet emotionally I struggled to believe that the very Creator who said to the oceans, "Here shall your proud waves stop" (Job 38:11), who stretched out the heavens, suspended the earth, and created billions of stars, actually *felt* love for me. I found it even more difficult to believe that this Almighty God, who rules the nations, could really *delight* in me.

I suppose I had always pictured God's love like a fountain. Shooting upward, it generously sprinkled down upon all who stood under it. It is the nature of a fountain to spout water; similarly, it is the nature of God to love. As wonderful as this over-flowing love was, it seemed almost generic, impersonal. But the love my sister referred to hinted of something much deeper, much more specific than "God is love" (1 John 4:8). This love she alluded to had the fragrance of something very tender, very intimate, very personal.

It's as if God unscrews the hose from the sprinkler and intentionally targets the water of His love, not merely into the air to shower all who run under it, but directly toward individuals. He purposely aims His love at *me*! He purposely directs His love to *you!* And just as a child on a hot summer day squeals with pure delight when pointing a hose at a friend and soaking him through his clothes, God rejoices with a shout of joy as He saturates each of us to the core. He *lavishes* upon us the riches of His grace (Ephesians 1:7–8).

Does it sound crazy that God not only loves us but also delights in us? Not according to His Word:

> *He will take great delight in you. . . . He will rejoice over you with shouts of joy!* (Zephaniah 3:17 NIV and NASB)

BELOVED CHILDREN

As my heart hoped this message of God's delight could be true, my mind argued. *It's too good to be true. Sure He loves me, but delights in me? Now that is pushing it.* Tolerates me *might be the more apt phrase to use. Maybe occasionally amused by, but* delight?

Several weeks later I strolled through an abbey in Northern England. Not usually drawn to icons, I casually walked past the many small wooden figures lining the stone walls—until one captured me. While tourists came and went, I stood entranced, meditating upon the Scripture and listening to God.

The representation portrayed Jesus at His baptism as John poured over Him waters from the Jordan. The Scripture above their heads read: "This is My Beloved Son in whom My soul delights" (Matthew 3:17).

Delight. There was that word again. The mysterious term that did not fit in my vocabulary about God—and most certainly did not fit in my vocabulary about myself. Feeling like I never quite pleased Him, I certainly could not imagine my delighting Him. Yet I had a sneaking suspicion God caught my eye with that icon for a reason; somehow He was speaking those words to me.

Well, certainly God could delight in Jesus, I contested with that flicker of hope—hope that it could actually be true. *Jesus was perfect. God* could *be pleased with one who obeyed Him perfectly. I don't. Jesus is His beloved Son. I am not.*

Just as that thought came, I remembered the words spoken to me as a new follower of Christ: "When God looks at you, He sees Jesus." Though it was beyond my limited understanding, I did believe that when God looks at me, He sees Christ's righteousness, not my sinfulness. Thus when God says He delights in Jesus, His beloved Son, perhaps—and this gave me a burst of hope—He could also delight in me. He could delight in me not because of anything I have done, but because of all that Jesus did on the cross.

The *Oxford Dictionary* defines delight in this way: "to give great pleasure or joy; to be greatly pleased." God does not merely tolerate us. Rather, now that we are in Christ, as my pastor reminded me, "His mouth drops over us!" God adores His children. The God of the universe actually gets just as tickled over us as a father does watching his child take her first steps. " 'Is Ephraim my dear son? Is he a delightful child? . . . Therefore My heart yearns for him; I will surely have mercy on him,' declares the Lord" (Jeremiah 31:20).

God calls us the "*apple* of His eye" (Zechariah 2:8, emphasis added)—the most tender, delicate part. We are precious to Him!

Julian of Norwich, a fourteenth-century mystic, recognized our difficulty embracing God's exuberant love for us:

> Do you know beyond all doubt that you are God's own child and you are loved by Him without measure? It is true. Your soul is loved, with a love so tender, by the One who is highest of all. His is a love so wonderful, far beyond anything we created beings can fully fathom.

Moreover, God feels delight for us as a loving husband feels toward his wife. He loves us not merely because He has betrothed himself to us—like a husband attempting to appease his wife by saying, "Of course I love you. I'm your husband"—love based merely upon a role. No, God's love beams with delight like the face of a groom seeing his bride walk down the aisle: "As the bridegroom rejoices over the bride, so your God will rejoice over you" (Isaiah 62:4–5).

C. S. Lewis captured this when he wrote,

> In an awful and surprising truth we are the objects of His love. You asked for a loving God, you've got one. Not a senile benevolence that drowsily wishes us all well in our own way. Not the cold philanthropy of a kind magistrate. But the consuming fire Himself. The love that made the worlds, persistent as the artist's love for her work, venerable as the father's love for his child, jealous, inexorable, exacting as love between the sexes.[1]

How can the knowledge of God's delight for us move from our heads to our hearts? Jesus said, "Unless you . . . become like children, you shall not enter the kingdom of heaven" (Matthew 18:3). As we become more childlike, embracing His delight, allowing ourselves to enjoy pleasure, to play, to laugh, and to rejoice, we taste more sweetly God's delight in us.

A GOD WHO SMILES

A few years after my walk through the abbey, I opened the door to the crisp January air and stepped outside to walk around the grounds of my new home. The overcast sky threatened more snow. Though excited to serve leaders and pastors through ministry at the retreat center where I had just started working, I felt gloomy like the gray skies. My heart missed home, family, friends—and I began second-guessing my decision to leave California and move to the mountains of Virginia.

Then I spotted it. An orange toboggan lying at the bottom of the sloping front lawn, looking as lonely as I felt. A sly smile pushed up the corners of my lips as I contemplated it—then tromped through the fresh fluffy snow, picked it up, and marched up the hill—my excitement barely outweighing my feelings of foolishness.

Jumping on, I rowed my way through the snow until, picking up speed, I soared down the hill. Landing in an embankment, my clothes covered in white and my spirit exhilarated, I felt ten years younger, and lighter. "That was great!" I exclaimed to God. As I looked up with a big smile, a thick ray of sunlight blazed through the dark clouds and shone right upon my face. Then, like a huge bright globe, the full sun emerged from between the clouds, blazing on me for a few moments. I had the distinct sense that God was smiling upon me, that as I took a risk to be childlike, to appear foolish before others, to play, God felt delight.

God smiling upon me? My favorite blessing in the Old Testament has always been the one God gave to Moses for the Israelites:

> *The Lord bless you, and keep you. The Lord make His face shine on you, and be gracious to you. The Lord lift up His countenance on you, and give you peace.* (Numbers 6:24–26)

But only recently did I learn, from a sermon by Reverend Earl Palmer, the full meaning of that blessing. *Barak* is the Hebrew word for "blessing." In the context of "[May] the Lord bless you, and keep you," it means, "May the Lord *stoop* toward you; [may] the Lord bend down and look into your face." In Hebrew, the phrase "May the Lord lift up His countenance" means *to smile.* So literally the verses mean, "May the Lord stoop toward you, bend down and look into your face, and smile upon you."

God smiles on us! We bring Him joy! "God formed us for His pleasure," writes A. W. Tozer, "and so formed us that we, as well as He, can, in divine communion, enjoy the sweet and mysterious mingling of kindred personalities. He meant us to see Him and live with Him and draw our life from His smile."[2]

I've often acted as if my hard work and serious determination somehow impressed God and made Him smile. Yet uptightness does not reflect God's character at all. G. K. Chesterton noted, "We have sinned and grown old. God is much younger than we." God does not look down on me with an expression of approval at how "seriously" I go about my business, as if the more intense I am, the more pleased He becomes. My very attempts to earn His smile often blindfold me from seeing His face. My drivenness hardens my heart to hearing His still, small whispers of love.

Parents light up when they watch their child giggle with delight. Even dog owners smile with contentment at the sight of their pet happily wagging its tail. How much more does God delight to see us joyful, peaceful, and smiling? My friend Jamie wrote me, describing her pleasure in overhearing her five-year-old son playing with his cousin: "While I was working and listening to them, I smiled and giggled to myself. I loved hearing and knowing his little voice. I loved that he's laughing. . . . I loved that he's enjoying himself!" God feels the same way about us!

Joy, I once read, is the most infallible sign of the presence of God. Joy flows from receiving God's smile. As we spend time in God's presence, we find fullness of joy (Psalm 16:11).

EXPERIENCING GOD IN PLEASURE

Could it be that one of the ways to experience God's delight in us more tangibly is to engage in things that give *us* delight? Could it be that what brings us joy and makes us smile brings joy and delight to our Father? Could it be that I *experience* His delight in me and with me as I take delight in God-given pleasure? Augustine wrote, "The things which by the help of your Spirit delight us are delighting you in us."[3]

Clearly the Designer of sexual intimacy between a husband and wife, the Creator of fragrant honeysuckle and wisteria, the Painter of purple sunsets, green parrots, and multicolored rainbows enjoys giving us pleasure. For in these we taste a glimpse of Him. "[God] is a hedonist at heart," wrote C. S. Lewis. "He has filled the world full of pleasures."[4]

King David exclaimed, "At Thy right hand are pleasures evermore" (Psalm 16:11 NKJV). *Could enjoying God-given delights be a wonderful means to deeper intimacy with Him? Could doing things we enjoy enable us to experience the presence and delight of God?*

Eric Liddell, an Olympic gold-medalist and missionary to China, loved to run. Describing his passion and joy, he stated, "When I run I feel God's pleasure." When we engage in that which brings us fulfillment, we feel the delight of God.

When I was a young believer, I used to feel like everything I did had to be *spiritual* for it to please God. If not apparently spiritual, I assumed it was not truly valuable. As my friends know, I love to dance—dance with everything in me, as it brings me great joy. I used to sometimes feel guilty for having so much fun in a seemingly non-spiritual activity. Now I see dancing as one of my most expressive ways to enjoy and praise God for the gift of life and of movement.

King David danced unabashedly, expressing praise at the return of the ark to Jerusalem (2 Samuel 6:16–23). Whom did God condemn in that incident? David for "leaping and dancing before the Lord"? Or his wife, Michal, who scowled from the sidelines at David's foolish abandon? God delights in our delight, and our delight brings praise to Him.

When we know God smiles upon us, we are liberated. We can relax in His love. We can rest in His care. We can live carefreely.

CAREFREE IN GOD

While I was at graduate school, one day—after spending most of it laboriously working on my master's thesis—I looked out my dorm window toward the grassy lawn. Being still for a moment, I sensed God's Spirit prompt me to put down my books and go out for a walk in the fresh spring air.

"No, I should stay here," I told myself. "I have so much research yet to do today."

The prompting persisted, so I negotiated. "Well, okay, I did want to get out and exercise."

Getting exercise was the one way I could justify a break. But as I started to walk briskly for a workout, I found myself listening to God: *"No, I want you to* stroll *with me, to stop and smell and look at the bright daffodils I have created for you, to listen to my Spirit through the lake, the birds, the green grass. Cast your cares upon me, my child, for I care for you. I will help you finish the work you need to do. Now is the time to take a break and visit with me."*

"But I feel like I am being careless and irresponsible in leaving my studies," I protested. As someone who tended to be overly conscientious, I had an aversion to anything resembling negligence.

Yet God persisted. *"I have not called you to be careless but* carefree. *You are full of so many worries about completing your master's degree. I want you to practice being carefree."*

Reluctantly, my feet slowed down. But as they did, my ears quickened to the sound of His voice. My eyes brightened at the sight of His presence all around me in His creation. During that simple, glorious walk with no big revelations, I enjoyed the quiet whispers of His care for me, and reminders through His creation to entrust the small details of my worries to Him. I walked back to my dorm.

As I reached for my key I realized I had dropped it somewhere on my walk.

"See, Lord," I said, "I *was* being careless. I knew I should have stayed in and studied. Now I am going to waste even more time trying to find my key."

I had so wanted to believe that it was His voice calling me to be carefree, but losing my key made me wonder if it was all my imagination—an excuse to be irresponsible and avoid my work. Criticizing myself, I wondered how I would ever find my key in the high grass and path that wound through the woods.

I sensed a gentle reminder from my heavenly Father: *"What does My Word say about casting* all *your cares upon me, about praying to me for all the details?"*

I prayed and began retracing my steps, surveying the area of daffodils where I had stopped and gazed, walking down by the lake, where I had prayed earlier. Nothing. Just as I started getting anxious, I sensed God again assuring me He cared about my concerns. I continued walking, and within moments the sunlight flashed on something brass in the grass by a flower patch—my key.

"Live carefree before God; He is most careful with you" (1 Peter 5:7 THE MESSAGE).

A GOD WHO CREATED LAUGHTER

When we are carefree in God, we are free to laugh. Laughter is clearly one of the most visible expressions of delight, of God's presence.

"One of the holiest women I have ever known did little with her life in terms of worldly success," writes Madeleine L'Engle. "[Her] gift was that of bringing laughter with her wherever she went, no matter how dark or grievous the occasion. Wherever she was, holy laughter was present to heal and redeem."[5]

Could it be that God is a lot more playful than we imagine? Could it be that He who created the neck of the ostrich, the hump of the camel's back, the tongue of the anteater, the feet of the platypus, might have a sense of humor? That He who created otters and dolphins that play in the ocean delights in seeing His creatures romp and frolic?

Laughter is the greatest antidote to taking ourselves too seriously. When I was working in China, I quickly realized the two most important tools for surviving and thriving in an unfamiliar culture were flexibility and a sense of humor. With prayer and laughter, we could get through anything. Though daily tempted with anxiety about all the unknowns, I discovered a secret: Humor disarms fear. Martin Luther wrote, "The devil cannot bear to be laughed at." And humor brings healing—in our relationships and to our souls and bodies. "A joyful heart is good medicine" (Proverbs 17:22).

God our Father delights to hear us laughing. As we allow ourselves to chuckle and play, to enjoy God-given pleasures, to sit like children on His lap, we experience the mystery of His delight in us. Henri Nouwen noted, "Every time you listen with great attentiveness to the voice that calls you the Beloved, you will discover within yourself a desire to hear that voice longer and more deeply."[6]

What does that voice sound like? For me, sometimes it is the voice of Scripture; sometimes it is heard in the words of a friend; sometimes in a hug on my leg from my two-year-old niece; sometimes it is a hummingbird sucking nectar from a flower near my window. As we take time for solitude, to nurture our spirit and relationship with God, to let Him love us, we better hear His words of love.

DELIGHTING IN GOD

What would it look like if we saw ourselves as radically loved by God—so much that He even goes wild-eyed over us with delight? We would eagerly come to Him, eagerly obey Him, eagerly delight in Him, and eagerly share His love with others.

After a church service, as I turned from the front of the sanctuary to walk down the aisle, my little three-year-old nephew, who had just finished Sunday school, spotted me. Throwing his arms up in the air, he squealed with delight, completely unaware of anyone else in the building, " 'Tacey!!" He propelled his little legs as fast as he could toward me and down the entire aisle of the church. I felt like the most important, valued, and honored person in the world at that moment. Sheer delight was written all over his wide-eyed face, heard in his gleeful voice, felt as he bounded toward me.

What if I responded to God in that way—realizing that no one and nothing else mattered when I caught a glimpse of Him? What if I held back not an ounce of my pure delight? How wonderful that would make Him feel! When we embrace God's delight in us, a spirit of delight flows from us toward God and toward others. We follow Him more closely because we want to be near Him. We obey Him more readily because we trust in His love. We freely give to others because we experience God's delight freely given to us.

When we embrace His delight over us we become relaxed and winsome—winsome witnesses for God. We radiate joy, abound with life, and emit grace.

Though it is a mystery to me why He actually delights in me, or any of us, He does. Whether through a bon voyage card, an icon at a retreat center, daffodils that laugh in the wind, a toboggan ride in the snow, or a still, small voice, God has continued to whisper, *"Let me love you. Let me delight in you. Don't resist my love or try to convince me of why I could not possibly delight in you. Let me do it, for it gives me joy. Receive it."*

THE MYSTERY OF DELIGHT: REFLECTIONS

QUESTIONS FOR JOURNAL AND/OR SMALL GROUP

1. Are you resisting God's love for you? How?
2. Would your life look different if you lived as if God truly delights and takes joy in you? In what ways?
3. What enables you to more fully experience God's delight?

4. What gives you delight? In what activity might you feel the pleasure of God?

5. Do one thing today or this week in which you take great delight (dance, create, climb, write, bake . . .).

VERSES TO TREASURE

The Lord takes pleasure in those who . . . hope in his steadfast love. (Psalm 147:11 NRSV)

You are precious in My sight . . . and I love you. (Isaiah 43:4)

The Lord appeared to him from afar, saying, "I have loved you with an everlasting love; therefore I have drawn you with lovingkindness" (Jeremiah 31:3).

It will no longer be said to you, "Forsaken," nor to your land will it any longer be said, "Desolate"; but you will be called "My delight is in her" and your land, "married" for the Lord delights in you and to Him your land will be married . . . As the bridegroom rejoices over the bride so your God will rejoice over you" (Isaiah 62:4–5).

THOUGHTS FOR CONTEMPLATION

"Laughter is the closest thing to the grace of God."
—Karl Barth, German theologian (1886–1968)

"The truth is that God is the most winsome of all beings and His service is one of unspeakable pleasure. He is all love, and those who trust Him need never know anything but that love."
—A. W. Tozer, *The Pursuit of God*

"Still the nagging, worrying voices that tell you to doubt your Lover's complete trustworthiness—and fix your thoughts on His good, lofty, and limitless compassion—so that you remain in His love."
—Julian of Norwich, *Daily Readings*

"The most wasted of all days is that during which one has not laughed."

—Nicolas de Chamfort, French playwright (1741–1794)

"When God almighty shares through His son the depth of His feelings for me, when His love flashes into my soul and when I am overtaken by Mystery . . . either I escape into skepticism or with radical amazement I surrender in faith to the truth of my belovedness.

"At every moment of our existence God offers us this good news. Sadly, many of us continue to cultivate such an artificial identity that the liberating truth of our belovedness fails to break through. So we become grim, fearful, and legalistic. We huff and puff to impress God, thrash about trying to fix ourselves, and live the gospel in such a joyless fashion that it has little appeal to nominal Christians and unbelievers searching for truth."

—Brennan Manning, *Abba's Child*

"The mass of men have been forced to be gay about the little things but sad about the big ones. Nevertheless I offer my last dogma [defiantly]: it is not native to man to be so. Man is more himself, man is more manlike, when joy is the fundamental thing in him and grief the superficial. Melancholy should be an innocent interlude—a tender and fugitive frame of mind. Praise should be the permanent pulsation of the soul. Pessimism is at best an emotional half holiday. Joy is the uproarious labor by which all things live.

"Joy which is the small publicity of the pagan is the gigantic secret of the Christian."

—G. K. Chesterton, *Orthodoxy*

HYMN: "Before the Throne of God"

Before the throne of God above,
I have one strong and perfect plea.
A great High Priest whose name is Love;

THE MYSTERY OF GOD'S DELIGHT / 167

Whoever lives and pleads for me.
My name is graven on His hands;
My name is written on His heart.
I know that while in heaven He stands
No tongue can bid me thence depart,
No tongue can bid me thence depart.

When Satan tempts me to despair
And tells me of the wrongs within,
Upward I look and see Him there,
Who made an end to all my sin.
Because the sinless Savior died,
My sinful soul is counted free.
For God, the Just is satisfied;
To look on Him and pardon me,
To look on Him and pardon me.

Behold him there! The Risen Lamb;
My perfect spotless Righteousness.
The great unchangeable I Am:
The King of Glory and of grace.
One with himself I cannot die;
My soul is purchased by His blood.
My life is hid with Christ on high;
With Christ my Savior and my God,
With Christ my Savior and my God.

MEDITATION

Be silent.
Be still.
Alone.
Empty
Before your God
Say nothing.
Ask nothing.
Be silent.
Be still.

Let your God
Look upon you.
That is all.
God knows.
God understands.
God loves you
With an enormous love,
And only wants
To look upon you
With that love.
Quiet.
Still.
Be.
Let your God—
Love you.

—Edwina Gateley, *Psalms of a Laywoman*

PRAYER SUGGESTION

"Pray, just as you are led, without reasoning, in all simplicity. Be a little child, hanging onto Him that loves you."

—John Wesley

10

BEING FULLY ALIVE:

THE MYSTERY OF LIFE

Mystery: There are mysteries which you can solve by taking thought. For instance, a murder-mystery whose mysteriousness must be dispelled in order for the truth to be known.

There are other mysteries which do not conceal a truth to think your way to, but whose truth is itself the mystery. The mystery of your self, for example. The more you try to fathom it, the more fathomless it is revealed to be. No matter how much of your self you are able to objectify and examine, the quintessential, living part of yourself will always elude you, i.e., the part that is conducting the examination. Thus, you do not solve the mystery, you live the mystery. And you do that not by fully knowing yourself but by fully being yourself.

Frederick Buechner, *Wishful Thinking*

The Glory of God is man fully alive.

St. Irenaeus of Lyons (A.D. 130–202)

I came that they might have life, and might have it abundantly.

John 10:10

A GROUP OF CENTENARIANS were asked, "If you had to live life over again, what would you change?" Each of them, from different backgrounds, races, and genders, replied, "I would risk more. Much more."

When we know, when we are convinced, when we begin to live the *truth* that we are God's precious, beloved children, redeemed in Christ, we become free—free to be the unique individuals God has created each of us to be. Free to risk. For when we know the truth, "the *truth* shall make [us] free" (John 8:32).

Describing a transforming experience of God's love, poet and author Maya Angelou writes,

> One day the teacher, Frederick Wilkerson, asked me to read to him. I was twenty-four, very erudite, very worldly. He asked that I read from *Lessons in Truth*, a section which ended with these words: "God loves me." I read the piece and closed the book, and the teacher said, "Read it again." I pointedly opened the book, and I sarcastically read, "God loves me." He said, "Again." After about the seventh repetition I began to sense that there might be truth in the statement, that there was a possibility that God really did love me. Me, Maya Angelou. I suddenly began to cry at the grandness of it all. *I knew that if God loved me, then I could do wonderful things, I could try great things, learn anything, achieve anything.* For what could stand against me with God, since one person, any person with God, constitutes the majority?[1]

When we know that God loves us, we *can* try anything. We can even dare to dream again after facing disappointments, broken dreams, and apparent failure.

A LIFE OF RISK

God is a God of risks. He risked the world in creating humans with free will. He had no guarantee that they would follow Him or follow the whims of their flesh. No guarantee they would use their hands to sew up or to inflict wounds, their mouths to bless or to belittle, their arms to cuddle or to bruise a baby. Yet He took the great risk by breathing life into our nostrils, and His Son took the great risk by dying even for those who would laugh at His name.

God calls us, too, to take risks. Throughout Scripture He calls His people to do what seems impossible, relying wholly upon Him through whom all things are possible.

In the parable of the talents, Jesus endorses the good stewards—the risk takers:

> For [the kingdom] is just like a man about to go on a journey, who called his own slaves, and entrusted his possessions to them. And to one he gave five talents, to another, two, and to another, one, each according to his own ability; and he went on his journey. Immediately the one who had received the five talents went and traded with them, and gained five more talents. In the same manner the one who had received the two talents gained two more. (Matthew 25:14–17)

THE PARABLE OF THE TALENTS

When the Master returned, he said to both stewards, "Well done, good and faithful slave; you were faithful in a few things, I will put you in charge of many things, enter into the joy of your master" (v. 21). He commended both stewards not on the basis of how much they made, for they had different talents and thus different returns on their investment. Rather, he congratulated them for their faithfulness in risking what he'd entrusted to them.

The third slave, however, buried his one talent in the ground, hiding his master's money (v. 18). He did the "safe" thing.

"No, it won't make any money," he rationalized to himself,

"but, at least I won't lose it. And hey, it's only one talent anyway. What can he expect from one talent? Better to be safe than sorry. . . ."

Too often I have shrunk back from taking a risk because it did not seem secure . . . because there were no guarantees . . . because I was not certain of what God wanted. But, as in the parable, it is *not* always better to be safe than sorry. "The desire for safety," observed the first-century historian Tacitus, "stands against every great and noble enterprise."

If we really want to live life abundantly, we will not live safely. We follow a God who calls us not to seek security but to seek first His kingdom at whatever cost. To lay down our lives. To follow what often seems ridiculous. To be willing to be misunderstood by the world, and at times even by those of faith.

In C. S. Lewis's *The Lion, the Witch, and the Wardrobe*, when Susan stumbled into the enchanting land with her brothers and sister, she asked Mrs. Beaver about the legendary Aslan, whom they are about to meet.

When Mrs. Beaver responded that Aslan was a lion, the King of Beasts, Susan replied,

> "Ooh! I thought he was a man. Is he—quite safe? I shall feel rather nervous about meeting a lion."
>
> "That you will, dearie, and no mistake," said Mrs. Beaver; "If there is anyone who can appear before Aslan without their knees knocking, they're either braver than most or else just silly."
>
> "Then he isn't safe?" said Lucy.
>
> "Safe?" said Mr. Beaver. "Don't you hear what Mrs. Beaver tells you? Who said anything about safe? 'Course he isn't safe. But He's good."[2]

We follow a God who is not safe, but something much better: utterly dependable and faithful. And only when we cast ourselves and all we have fully into His hands are we truly secure. Fear often causes us to shrink back from the risk of obedience.

"I was afraid and went away and hid your talent in the ground," exclaimed the lazy steward to the master.

"But his master said to him: 'You wicked lazy slave. . . . You ought to have put my money in the bank, and on my arrival I would have received my money back with interest. Therefore, take away the talent from him, and give it to the one who has the ten . . . and cast out the worthless slave into the outer darkness' " (Matthew 25:26–30).

Like this man, when fear of risk, fear of doing the "wrong" thing overtakes me, I settle for the *safe* thing—that which I know (or think I know) God approves (that which appears spiritual or sacrificial). But throughout Scripture, God commends—and requires—risk, even in the midst of uncertainty: Abraham moving to a land he's never known; Noah building an ark under sunny skies; Joshua attacking a land of giants; the mother of Moses sending her baby in a basket down the Nile; David initiating battle with a behemoth; Esther risking her life on behalf of the Israelites. Throughout His ministry Jesus often exhorted His followers to not be afraid: "Be not afraid, only believe" (Mark 5:36 KJV).

Fear is like a curve ball in tennis. The tendency for a beginning player, when a curve ball comes spinning over the net, is to step *back* to hit the ball. Yet she must do just the opposite and move directly *in to* the ball. The longer she hesitates, the more out of control the ball spins. When fears come at us, rather than backing up in an attempt to brace ourselves, we need to charge directly into them, conquering them before they conquer us.

As we believe and obey what God is calling us to do, no matter how scary it may feel, we come to know Him more intimately. "He who has my commandments and keeps them," Jesus taught his disciples, "he it is who loves Me . . . and I will love him, and will disclose Myself to him" (John 14:21).

Though there may be many things we *don't* know—many questions for which we have no answers—we can dwell on and

[handwritten margin note: God speaks thru - Word - prompting - specified calling]

obey what we *do* know: what He has spoken to us through His Word, a prompting, or a specific calling. As we begin to obey what we do know, to live by what we do know, we experience new heights and depths in our relationship with God. Oswald Chambers observed,

> All God's revelations are sealed until they are opened to us by obedience. You will never get them open by philosophy or thinking. Immediately if you obey, a flash of light comes. Obey God in the thing He shows you, and instantly the next thing is opened up. It is not study that does it, but obedience. The tiniest fragment of obedience, and heaven opens and the profoundest truths of God are yours straight away. God will never reveal more truth about Himself until you have obeyed what you already know.[3]

As we obey what we know, we experience the thrill of becoming more fully alive, more truly the person God intended us to be, and, ultimately, more like Christ.

A woman whom I heard speak asked Mother Teresa in Calcutta, "*How* can you do this—working in the slums?"

Mother Teresa responded, beaming, "It's *pure joy.*"

[handwritten margin note: Being fully alive is consequence to obedience] Pure joy. When we do what God has called us to, whether a seemingly minor step of obedience or a major life change, we experience the rapturous delight of being fully alive. Though obedience may require (or appear to require) the sacrifice of temporal happiness, in due time we gain joy—deeper, wider, broader, more lasting than any bout of happiness. "Keep my commandments," said Jesus, "that My joy may be in you, and that your joy may be made full" (John 15:10–11).

RISKING THROUGH UNCERTAINTY

But what about when God's directives are not so clear? When the promptings of the Spirit are not so recognizable? More often than not when I face decisions, I grope for direction. When deciding in which of three foreign countries to attend graduate school, knowing my choice would affect the future direction of my life, I pleaded for God's guidance. I worked myself into such anxiety about my decision that I was miserable—to myself and, I am sure, to those around me. Finally, as I continued to seek an answer—"God, what do you want me to do?"—I sensed His reminding me that I was neglecting the very things around me I *knew* He wanted me to do—to wholly trust Him, to cast my anxiety upon Him, to faithfully serve while still at my job, to be attentive to my roommate.

Another time, as I wrestled with whether or not to continue working at a particular job, I fretfully asked God to show me what He wanted me to do. After much angst, I sensed His admonishing me, *"Stacey, you are so worried about making a mistake, making a 'wrong' decision. What does my Word say? 'Lo, I am with you always.' I will not forsake you. Trust that I will be with you whatever way you choose."*

I then recalled deliberating about a decision I'd made years before to visit John in Africa. Unlike other choices, I had only a few days in which to equivocate before I would lose my reservation for the last seat on the plane. As I prayed for wisdom, out of nowhere, Martin Luther's words came to mind: *"Go and sin boldly."*

I had heard that once before but was not quite sure what Luther meant. Yet this time, it seemed clear: I had to make a decision. Without sensing the Lord leading me one way or the other, there was no guarantee that whatever I chose would be the *right* move. I had to risk the possibility of making a *wrong* decision. But whatever direction I chose—in this decision and other more important decisions that seemed unclear—I had to go boldly, to risk boldly like the good stewards.

Could it be that perhaps the Lord grants us much more freedom—freedom to try, to risk, to dream, to experience—than we embrace due to fear? Paul tells us, "Where the Spirit of the Lord is, there is liberty" (2 Corinthians 3:17). Rather than becoming paralyzed by the talent in our hand, or burying it in a safe place, we can go forward boldly, even at the risk of not doing the "right" thing, even without assurance that this is the best place to invest ourselves.

Solomon, known as the wisest king in the world, said, "Sow your seed in the morning, and do not be idle in the evening, for you do not know whether morning or evening sowing will succeed, or whether both of them alike will be good" (Ecclesiastes 11:6). Planting requires risk. There is no guarantee when, or if, seed will produce fruit. But sow anyway, morning and evening, even when there is no guarantee of the outcome, even at the threat of loss or failure. For "he who watches the wind will not sow and he who looks at the clouds will not reap" (Ecclesiastes 11:4). If we wait for total assurance, we will rarely risk—and rarely harvest.

SAYING NO TO SELF-LIMITATIONS

"Argue for your limitations long enough and, sure enough, they're yours."

—Richard Bach

My father has often reminded me that most of our limits (apart from physical incapacities) are self-imposed. "Don't close your own doors," he would respond when I explained I was not applying for a particular graduate school or job since I assumed I was underqualified.

When we limit ourselves, we limit God. When I felt prompted to write *Living With Mystery*, my first response to Him was, "I can't write a book! I have no idea how to write it, what to say, who would want to read it." I made excuses for several years, until the Spirit convicted me that when I say, "I can't do it!" I am really saying to God, "You are unable to do that through me."

Yet God responds to our fears, as He did with Moses, who voiced his lack of eloquence. He says, "The issue isn't whether or not *you* can do it; the issue is that I plan to do it through you. Thus, you *will* be able to do it regardless if you think you can't." He is the One who accomplishes all things for us (Psalm 57:2).

We serve a God who delights to do the impossible, a God with whom all things are possible (Matthew 19:26), a God for whom nothing is too difficult (Jeremiah 32:27). Do we really believe that? When was the last time we attempted something that could not be done apart from the help of God, something that seemed an impossibility to us?

In fact, when something seems possible by our own means, God often takes away the very means we rely upon so He can do the impossible through us. When God called Gideon to fight the Midianites, Gideon recruited 32,000 people to fight. In Gideon's mind, those 32,000 seemed like nothing compared to the 120,000 warriors of the enemy. Yet the Lord responded, "The people who are with you are too many for Me to give Midian into their hands, lest they become boastful, saying, 'My own power has delivered me' " (Judges 7:2). The Lord whittled Gideon's army down to 300 men! Yet by His power, those 300 men attacked and defeated over 120,000 warriors, initially using only trumpets, torches, and pitchers.

I wanted to do something adventurous immediately after graduating from college, but when God opened a door for me to teach in China, I thought, *No way! I can't teach. I have no experience. I am too young to instruct university students. I don't know a thing about China, I don't speak a word of Chinese, nor do I have an appetite for the Chinese delicacy—chickens' feet!* However, trusting that God was greater than all my fears, I finally stepped forward. That year turned out to be the most fulfilling and richly blessed year of my life.

Letting go of our inhibitions requires risk. Being fully alive demands daring. But when we know the truth that nothing can separate us from God's love, that our identity lies in Christ alone, we are set free. Free to be all that we were created to be. Free to obey the movement of the Spirit within us—our hearts, our minds, our dreams—even when that movement leads us to do something foolish or impossible in the eyes of others.

Jesus saves us not only *from* spiritual death, but *to* spiritual life—so that we may truly live! As I read one day about martyrs for the faith, fear and guilt overcame me. *Oh, Lord,* I confessed, *I don't know for certain that if under terrifying physical torture, I would be willing to die for you.*

I sensed God interrupt my anguished thoughts: *"Stacey, don't be so worried about whether or not you would be willing to die for me. More importantly, I want you to live for me."* "To *live* is Christ" (Philippians 1:21).

DREAMING

Faithfully being the unique person God has created us to be, being fully alive, includes following the dreams and passions He has written on our hearts.

I used to hesitate to dream, wondering, *What if I dream something that is not God's plan for me? Shouldn't I only be concerned with obeying what God's Word says for me to do?* Yet as I grow in my relationship with God and experience His love that has come to set us free, I realize I delight Him when I take risks to pursue the dreams He's given me.

Solomon writes, "Rejoice . . . and follow the impulses of your heart . . . knowing that He will bring you to judgment for all these things" (Ecclesiastes 11:9). We are encouraged to follow our deepest passions, always bearing in mind the account of our lives we'll give Him on the final day. God grants us freedom, as He told the Israelites, to enjoy "whatever your heart desires" (Deuteronomy 14:26) as we walk in obedience to Him. Augustine put it succinctly when he said, "Love God and do as you please." When we truly love the Lord, we are free to pursue our dreams, for in all we do we will seek to please and honor Him.

What if I fail? When we begin following a dream or a prompting He has placed on our heart, we need not worry about the outcome. A man observing Mother Teresa marveled how she poured herself into serving the sick when hundreds were literally dying around her. He asked how she could persevere when her efforts appeared statistically unsuccessful—for when compared to the number who died, relatively few lived. Mother Teresa responded, "God does not call me to be successful. He calls me to be faithful."

What about broken dreams? For me, even scarier than failing, is dreaming again after experiencing many dreams broken. During the darkest times of my illness, dreaming was the farthest thing from my mind. Not only dreams, but even everyday activities I had taken for granted—working full time, living on my own, exercising, socializing—were unrealizable.

Yet I could still risk . . . risk by trusting God when circumstances shouted not to. Risk by following the promptings on my heart to begin writing, even when I knew not why, what, or for whom. Risk to pray for and write a letter to encourage someone as God led me. Though seemingly insignificant, during the times of continuing disappointment, these were the tiny steps of risk I could take.

When Tim Hansel, a mountain climber, suffered a near-fatal fall during an expedition, his doctors told him he would live with excruciating pain the rest of his life. Though he battled intense physical and emotional suffering, he wrote in his journal of his will to embrace life even in the midst of great pain: "Each morning new hope. Life is more difficult, and at times strangely more delicious than it's ever been. *I will continue to* choose *to make it so.*"[4]

HE IS OUR LIFE (Colossians 3:4)

Being fully alive means embracing *all* of life—in all its mystery, all its pain, all its joy, all its agony, all its glory. And as we fully embrace life, we come to know God better, not only in the light but also in the dark; not only in the answers but also in the questions; not only in the joys but also in the sorrows.

The deeper spiritual life is not about questions being answered, pain being anesthetized, dreams being realized, limitations being conquered, or longings being fulfilled. It's about knowing and worshiping God. For therein lies our life—abundant life.

THE MYSTERY OF LIFE: REFLECTIONS

QUESTIONS FOR JOURNAL AND/OR SMALL GROUP

1. What would you do if you were not afraid? What would you do if you knew you could not fail?
2. When do you feel most alive? Do something that makes you feel alive this week (drawing, dancing, singing, playing, journaling, hiking, writing a letter)—no matter how small.
3. List your dreams. Include both the apparently wild and the seemingly mundane.
4. Recall a time when you took a great risk and how God was faithful through it.
5. What is a small risk or step you can take *today*?
6. What is a greater risk you can take this week, month, or year?
7. What is something God has been prompting you to be obedient in? What is something he may be nudging you to say *yes!* to?

VERSES TO TREASURE

I have set before you life and death, the blessing and the curse. So choose life in order that you may live, you and your descendants, by loving the Lord your God, by obeying His voice, and by holding fast to Him. (Deuteronomy 30:19–20, emphasis added)

How long will you put off entering to take possession of the land which the Lord, the God of your fathers, has given you? . . . Therefore, be strong and courageous! Do not tremble or be dismayed, for the Lord your God is with you wherever you go. (Joshua 18:3; 1:9)

Do not fear, for I am with you; do not anxiously look about you, for I am your God. I will strengthen you, surely I will help you, surely I will uphold you with My righteous right hand. (Isaiah 41:10)

For God has not given us a spirit of timidity, but of power and love and discipline. (2 Timothy 1:7)

"If you can!" All things are possible to him who believes. (Mark 9:23)

THOUGHTS FOR CONTEMPLATION

"Whatever you can do, or dream you can, begin it. Boldness has genius, power, and magic in it."

—Goethe

"Nothing great is accomplished with caution."

—Ralph Waldo Emerson

"If we did all that we are capable of doing, we would literally astound ourselves."

—Thomas Edison

"All things are possible until they are proved impossible— and even the impossible may only be so, as of now."

—Pearl Buck

POETRY

Teach me, my God and King,
in all things thee to see,
and what I do in any thing,
to do it as for thee.
  —George Herbert, seventeenth-century English poet and
                                                    clergyman

i thank You God for this most amazing day:
for the leaping greenly spirits of trees
and a blue true dream of sky; and for everything
which is natural which is infinite which is yes
(i who have died am alive again today,
and this is the sun's birthday; this is the birth
day of life and of love and wings: and of the gay
great happening illimitably earth)
how should tasting touching hearing seeing
breathing any—lifted from the no
of all nothing—human merely being
doubt unimaginably You?
(now the ears of my ears awake and
now the eyes of my eyes are opened)
                                              —e e cummings

FURTHER THOUGHTS

"I went to the woods because I wanted to live deliberately, to suck the marrow from the bones of life; to put to rout all that was not life, and not to come to the end of life, and discover that I had not lived."

—Henry David Thoreau

"Life is God's greatest gift to us and yet is bounded by time in the form of the present moment. We shall only pass this particular way once, at this particular moment. What we do not say, do not do, remains forever unsaid, undone. The word of love, the deed of kindness, the opportunity missed, never returns—at least not in a precisely identical form.

"Jesus stresses so much this preciousness. There is only today in which to trust the Father, to let him provide for us, while we seek him through loving and serving our neighbor. We have to seize opportunities that lie at hand.

"To live as a child is to live fully in the present."

—Elizabeth Ruth Obbard, *Magnificat:*
The Journey and the Song

"The old prayer speaks of God 'in whose service is perfect freedom.' The paradox is not as opaque as it sounds. It means that to obey Love himself, who above all else wishes us well, leaves us the freedom to be the best and gladdest that we have it in us to become. The only freedom Love denies us is the freedom to destroy ourselves."

—Frederick Buechner, *Wishful Thinking:*
A Theological ABC

"For all that has been—Thanks! For all that will be—Yes!"

—Dag Hammarskjöld, *Markings*

PRAYER

Lord, I want to live life holding nothing back. Help me to live from the depths of my soul and not from my fears of appearing foolish before others. To say, "Get behind me!" to self-imposed limitations. "Be gone!" to worry and what-ifs.

Help me to say no! to fears and yes! to you. . . . Yes to dream; yes to wonder; yes to seize the day; yes to try and fail, to laugh and try again! Yes to embrace life with all its uncertainties and to do what I have uniquely been gifted to do.

Thank you for the amazing gracious gift of life. Trusting you, I will seize this day, this once-in-a-lifetime gift I have been given.

EPILOGUE

For now we see in a mirror dimly, but then face to face; now I know in part, but then I shall know fully just as I have been fully known.

1 Corinthians 13:12

EVER SINCE I LEARNED to talk I have liked to ask questions. And though I've found value in the questions, I cannot deny that I desire, and hope for, answers. Periodically I make a list of queries in my mind and go to meet with my pastor to ask him for answers. I walk into his office with my note pad ready, expecting to go down the list, checking off each question, and filling in the blanks.

But the reality is, after walking into his office, I take off my coat, sit down in the high-backed chair, and we talk. I voice my struggles, my wrestling, my questions. He adds his thoughts, talks of his experiences, and listens deeply.

I walk away with a few notes jotted, but the blanks still empty. I do not get all my questions answered or the blanks filled in, but I receive something better: companionship in my grappling, empathy in my confusion, sharing in life's stories and struggles. I walk out feeling lighter in spirit, less fixated on the questions, more at ease in the not knowing because my pastor has sat beside me in my wrestling. In fact, perhaps I am secretly relieved that my questions were *not* all answered. For more than answers to questions one through ten, I needed someone to be with me in the midst of the mystery.

This side of eternity, rather than tick off our checklist of questions and fill in our blanks, God welcomes us into His office, pulls up a chair, motions us to make ourselves comfortable, and sits with us. Listens to us. Aches with us. Even cries with us. And it's okay—it's going to be okay. Even though our questions remain unanswered; even though we wrestle with the mysteries of suffering, darkness, pain, unfulfillment, brokenness; even though we fear being honest with God, others, and ourselves, fear risking and embracing life with all its mystery, God is with us. He reaches out and embraces us. Holds us. Comforts us. It's going to be okay, for it's not so much answers we really need—it's God himself.

Whether we realize it or not, He is what we've really come for. When we meet Him in eternity, our questions will be answered, our brokenness made whole, our longings fulfilled, our sorrows turned to joy. But for now, while our blanks remain blank and our questions unanswered, He abides with us. He feels with us. He promises that as we walk by faith, entrusting our questions, our mysteries, and our lives to Him, He will walk beside us into eternity when "all now mysterious shall be bright at last." Now, as we live the mystery, we come to know Him as we have never known Him before. One day, we will fully embrace the Answer—and He will never let us go.

ADDITIONAL RESOURCES

MYSTERY OF HONESTY

"What matters supremely, therefore, is not, in the last analysis, the fact that I know God, but the larger fact which underlies it—the fact that *He knows me*. I am graven on the palms of His hands. I am never out of His mind. All my knowledge of Him depends on His sustained initiative in knowing me. I know Him because He first knew me, and continues to know me. He knows me as a friend, one who loves me; and there is no moment when His eye is off me, or His attention distracted from me, and no moment, therefore, when His care falters.

"This is momentous knowledge. There is unspeakable comfort—the sort of comfort that energizes, be it said, not enervates—in knowing that God is constantly taking knowledge of me in love, and watching over me for my good. There is tremendous relief in knowing that God's love to me is utterly realistic, based at every point on prior knowledge of the worst about me, so that no discovery can disillusion Him about me, in the way I am so often disillusioned about myself, or quench His determination to bless me. There is, certainly, great cause for humility in the thought that he sees all the twisted things about me that my fellowmen do not see (and I am glad!), and that He sees more corruption in me than that which I see in myself (which, in all conscience, is enough). There is, however, equally great incentive to worship and love God in the thought that, for some unfathomable reason, He wants me as His friend, and desires to be my friend, and has given His Son to die for me in order to realize this purpose."

—J. I. Packer, *Knowing God*

MYSTERY OF LOVE

"It may be possible for each to think too much of his own potential glory hereafter; it is hardly possible for him to think too often or too deeply about that of his neighbor. The load, or weight, or burden of my neighbor's glory should be laid on my back daily, a load so heavy that only humility can carry it. It is a serious thing to live in a society of possible gods and goddesses, to remember the dullest and most uninteresting person you can talk to may one day be a creature, which if you saw him now, you would be strongly tempted to worship, or else a horror as you now meet, if at all, only in a nightmare. All day long we are, in some degree, helping each other to one or the other of these destinations. It is therefore in light of these overwhelming possibilities, it is with the proper amount of awe and circumspection, that we should conduct all of our dealings with one another, all friendships, all loves, all play, all politics. There are no *ordinary* people. You have never talked to a mere mortal. Nations, cultures, arts, civilizations—these are mortal, and their life is to our life as the life of a gnat. But it is immortals with whom we joke, work, marry, snub, and exploit—immortal horrors or everlasting splendors.

"Next to the Blessed Sacrament itself, your neighbor is the

holiest object presented to your senses. If he is your Christian neighbor, he is holy in almost the same way, for in him also Christ—the glorifier and the glorified, Glory Himself, is truly hidden."

—C. S. Lewis, *The Weight of Glory*

MYSTERY OF BROKENNESS

Go Into the Place of Your Pain

"You have to live through your pain gradually and thus deprive it of its power over you. Yes, you must go into the place of your pain, but only when you have gained some new ground. When you enter your pain simply to experience it in its rawness, it can pull you away from where you want to go.

"What is your pain? It is the experience of not receiving what you most need. It is a place of emptiness where you feel sharply the absence of the love you most desire. To go back to that place is hard, because you are confronted there with your wounds as well as with your powerlessness to heal yourself. You are so afraid of that place that you think of it as a place of death. Your instinct for survival makes you run away and go looking for something else that can give you a sense of at-homeness, even though you know full well that it can't be found out in the world.

"You have to begin to trust that your experience of emptiness is not the final experience, that beyond it is a place where you are being held in love. As long as you do not trust that place beyond your emptiness, you cannot safely reenter the place of pain.

"So you have to go into the place of your pain with the knowledge in your heart that you have already found the new place. You have already tasted some of its fruits. The more roots you have in the new place, the more capable you are of mourning the loss of the old place and letting go of the pain that lies there. You cannot mourn something that has not died. Still, the old pains, attachments, and desires that once meant so much to you need to be buried.

"You have to weep over your lost pains so that they can gradually leave you and you can become free to live fully in the new place without melancholy or homesickness."

—Henri Nouwen, *The Inner Voice of Love*

MYSTERY OF LIMITATIONS

"A water bearer in India had two large pots, one hanging on each end of a pole he carried across his neck. While one pot was perfect and always delivered a full portion of water at the end of the long walk from the stream to the master's house, the other pot had a crack, and it arrived only half full of water.

"For a full two years this went on daily, with the bearer delivering only one and a half pots full of water to his master's house. Of course, the perfect pot was proud of its accomplishments, perfect to the end for which it was made. But the poor cracked pot was ashamed of its imperfection, and miserable that it was able to accomplish only half of what it had been made to do. After two years of what it perceived to be a bitter failure, it spoke to the water bearer one day by the stream. 'I am ashamed of myself, and I want to apologize to you.'

" 'Why?' asked the bearer. 'What are you ashamed of?'

" 'I have been able, for these past two years, to deliver only half my load because this crack in my side causes water to leak out all the way back to your master's house,' the pot said. 'Because of my flaws, you have to do all of this work, and you don't get full value from your efforts.'

"The water bearer felt sorry for the old cracked pot, and in his compassion he replied, 'As we return to the master's house, I want you to notice the beautiful flowers along the path.' Indeed, as they went up the hill, the old cracked pot took notice of the sun warming the beautiful wild flowers on the side of the path, and this cheered it some.

"But at the end of the trail, it still felt bad because it had leaked out half its load, and so again it apologized to the bearer for its failure.

"The bearer said to the pot, 'Did you notice that there were flowers only on your side of your path, but not on the other pot's side? That's because I have always known about your flaw, and I took advantage of it. I planted flower seeds on your side of the path, and every day while we walk back from the stream, you've watered them. For two years I have been able to pick these beautiful flowers to decorate my master's table. Without you being just the way you are, he would not have this beauty to grace his house.' "

—Source unknown

MYSTERY OF DARKNESS

HELPS FOR PRAYING WHILE IN PAIN AND SUFFERING[1]

1. *Save me, O God. . . . I am weary with my crying; my throat is parched.* (Psalm 69:1, 3)

When you have difficulty formulating words to pray, read through the Psalms and pray along with David and the other psalmists. I have found the following psalms to be especially helpful during times of pain and darkness: 6, 10, 13, 22, 30, 31, 40, 42, 55, 56, 69, 71, 84, 88, 118, and 145.

2. *Pour out your heart before Him.* (Psalm 62:8)

Be completely transparent with God about your feelings, struggles, and pain. Though He knows it all, when we are vulnerable before Him our intimacy with Him deepens.

3. *Be assured that God's purpose, even in times of testing, is "to do good for you in the end"* (Deuteronomy 8:16).

Daily surrender your suffering to God. Pray that His purposes would be accomplished and that He would be glorified through your suffering. Believe that He works all adversity both for His glory and our good as we accept everything from His hand.

4. *The law of the Lord is perfect, restoring the soul.* (Psalm 19:7)

Ask God to guide you to specific promises in His Word that will speak to your pain and will sustain you during this time.

5. *Lord, I believe. Help Thou mine unbelief.* (Mark 9:24 KJV)

Confess areas in which you are doubting God and His promises. Ask for faith to believe His Word.

6. *The Spirit also helps our weakness; for we do not know how to pray as we should, but the Spirit Himself intercedes for us with groaning too deep for words.* (Romans 8:26)

When you are at a loss for words but heavy in heart, ask the Holy Spirit to pray for you in ways you are unable to.

7. *He always lives to make intercession for them.* (Hebrews 7:25)

Ask Jesus to intercede for you. Ask God to raise up intercessors for you and to put you on their hearts when you most need prayer support. Take time to intercede for others as Jesus and others are doing for you.

8. *I am afflicted and in pain. . . . I will praise the name of God with song.* (Psalm 69:29–30)

Listen to and sing worship music that will remind you of His love and power.

9. *The Lord gave and the Lord has taken away. Blessed be the name of the Lord.* (Job 1:21)

Though many questions may remain unanswered about your suffering, begin praising the Lord for what you do know: that He is good (Psalm 119:68), that He is in control (1 Chronicles 29:11), and that nothing can separate you from His love (Romans 8:39).

THOUGHTS FOR CONTEMPLATION

"If he sends us happiness let us accept it gratefully. Like the Good Shepherd he sets us in a rich pasture to strengthen us to follow him later into barren lands. If he sends us crosses, let us embrace them and say, '*Bona Crux,*' for this is the greatest grace of all. It means walking through life hand in hand with our Lord, helping him to carry his Cross like Simon of Cyrene. It is our Beloved asking us to prove how much we love him. Whether in mental suffering or bodily pain 'let us rejoice and tremble with joy.' Our Lord calls us and asks us to tell him of our love and repeat it over and over again all through our sufferings.

"Every cross, great or small, even small annoyances, are the voice of the Beloved. He is asking for a declaration of love from us to last whilst the suffering lasts. . . . Your will be done, my Brother Jesus, and not mine. We long to forget ourselves, we ask nothing, only your glory."

—Charles de Foucauld, *Meditations of a Hermit*

"Moses approached the thick darkness where God was" (Exodus 20:21 NIV).

"God has still His hidden secrets, hidden from the wise and prudent. Do not fear them; be content to accept things that you cannot understand; wait patiently. Presently He will reveal to you the treasures of darkness, the riches of the glory of the mystery. Mystery is only the veil of God's face.

"Do not be afraid to enter the cloud that is settling down on your life. God is in it. The other side is radiant with His glory. 'Think it not strange concerning the fiery trial which is to try you, as though some strange thing happened unto you; but rejoice, in as much as ye are partakers of Christ's suffering.' When you seem loneliest and most forsaken, God is night. He is in the dark cloud. Plunge into the blackness of its darkness without flinching; under the shrouding curtain of His pavilion you will find God awaiting you."

—Mrs. Charles E. Cowman, *Streams in the Desert*

"These troubles and distresses that you go through in these Waters are not signs that God hath forsaken you, but are sent to try you, whether you will call to mind that which heretofore you have received of his goodness, and live upon him in your distresses.

"Then I saw in my Dream that Christian was as in a muse a while. To whom also Hopeful added this word, Be of good cheer, Jesus Christ maketh thee whole: and with that Christian brake out with a loud voice, Oh, I see him again, and he tells me, When thou passest through the Waters, I will be with thee: and through the Rivers, they shall not overflow thee. Then they both took courage, and the Enemy was after that as still as a stone, until they were gone over. Christian, therefore, presently found ground to stand upon, and so it followed that the rest of the River was but shallow. Thus they got over."

—John Bunyan, *The Pilgrim's Progress*

PRAYER FROM THE PIT—JOSEPH'S CRY

Why am I here, Lord?
Darkness blinds me.
Fear envelops me.
Despair submerges my head.
O, Lifter of my head,
raise me from this pit of darkness,
this cave of despair.
I have been torn from my loved ones,
betrayed by my brethren,
separated from all that is good and promise-filled.
My eyes grope for rays of light from
an opening above . . .
but only blackness laughs back at me.
Where are you, Lord?
You promised never to leave me nor forsake me.
You gave me a dream—of hope, of glory, of purpose.
Yet, you have allowed me to be cast into the pit.
I don't understand.
I cry out to you.

Yet, only my weary voice echoes to me
from the cold walls.
Hear my cry, O God;
listen to my prayer.
From the ends of the earth I call to you,
I call as my heart grows faint.
When my soul can sob no longer,
When the depths of my pain and isolation
have wrung my body limp,
When I am too weak to utter another cry,
Then it is silent . . .
I am silent.
And in the silence,
I hear you.
I discover you are here with me,
and have been all along.
Truly, if I make my bed in the Sheol,
behold, Thou art there.
Even this, Thou hast meant for good.
Though my enemy intended it for evil,
Thou hast meant it for good.

MYSTERY OF SOLITUDE AND SILENCE

TAKING A SPIRITUAL RETREAT[2]

One of the most rewarding ways of practicing silence and
solitude as a means to deepening our intimacy with God is
through taking a personal spiritual retreat. Following are some
suggestions on how to plan and implement one.

Where do I go?

Though you can take a spiritual retreat anywhere you can
find solitude—even a quiet corner of your backyard or a park—
I recommend at some point planning one at a convent, monastery, or other retreat center.

Over the past thirteen years, I have visited a wide variety of retreat centers—from a simple abbey in the countryside where cloistered nuns resided, to a large former mansion in an orange grove where guests ate gourmet dinners. When I have little time to get away, I've visited a retreat conference center where I can enjoy quiet solitude with God within a half-hour's drive from my home. In most retreat centers, rooms are very simple and bathrooms often shared. Yet regardless of the size or location of a retreat center, the quiet spiritual atmosphere there (as opposed to staying at a hotel) helps me focus upon God.

However, if you are unable to stay at a retreat center, perhaps a friend has a cabin or home away from a populated area that you could use for a few days of solitude. I seek locations where I can avoid the temptation to interact with others, run errands, etc. I especially enjoy places where I can take walks in nature.

What do I bring?

Pack light. I recommend bringing a Bible, a journal, and perhaps a devotional guide or reflective book on deepening intimacy with God. Pack your most comfortable clothes, an extra sweater (some rooms may be drafty), slippers, shoes for walking/hiking, and a towel or blanket to sit on outside if weather permits.

Before leaving, ask friends and family to pray for you during your retreat that God would help you to be still before Him, enable you to listen to His voice, and draw you into deeper intimacy with Him.

How long should I plan to stay?

I often find it takes me two to three days to quiet my spirit and truly become still enough to listen. Yet if you can initially spare only a few hours for a retreat, even that is a great place to start. It's easy to get antsy at such a drastic change of pace and activity from our daily lives. In fact, after the first two or three days, you may experience a great temptation to flee the silence and return to activity. However, I've found that when I resist my urge to leave, God often reveals to me some deeper truths about Him, and myself, helping me to know Him in a fresh way. Some of my greatest times communing with God have come only *after* I have resisted the urge to "cut and run."

What should I expect when I arrive?

You may head into your time on retreat with specific issues or pending decisions you want to talk with God about while there, but try to leave any agenda at home. He may want to address something totally different than what is on your mind— something that only after waiting upon Him and asking what's on *His* mind will you understand. Let go of your expectations of receiving a word from God, getting an area of your life totally resolved, or having a "burning bush" experience. God may reveal unexpected, amazing things—or He may just want to stoke your love and desire for Him and show you the simple joy of sitting at His feet. A retreat is not necessarily a time for mountaintop revelations, but a time to nurture your relationship with God—time to be alone with Him.

What do I do now that I am here?

I like to start my retreat with a walk around the grounds, praying that God would open my heart to His plans and open my ears to His still, small voice. As I walk, I also ask God to show me what I can learn about Him from His creation. I have found that just as Jesus often taught in parables about fig trees, sparrows, and mountains, God often teaches us through His creation. I carry my journal with me to record reflections along the way. I also keep a lookout for pleasant places to sit so that I can return there later with a book to read or sketchbook to draw in.

One of my favorite rewards on retreat is having long, uninterrupted blocks of time to read Scripture—one of the few times I can enjoy reading through a book of the New or Old Testament in one sitting. If a verse or passage especially speaks to me, I write it on a file card and enjoy time to memorize and meditate upon it as I stroll the grounds. Or perhaps I'll do a word study in the Bible on an area in which I need encouragement (such as hope or trials) or on an attribute of God's character (like goodness, compassion, faithfulness). I also sometimes enjoy listening to a sermon tape while walking the grounds.

At some retreat centers, the sisters, monks, or retreat staff hold various types of prayer meetings (such as contemplative prayer, *Lectio Divina*, or chanting the Psalms) in which all retreatants are welcome. Also at many centers "spiritual directors" (those trained to help you determine how God is at work in your life) can meet with you to offer counsel and/or prayer during your retreat.

After lunch I enjoy a delightful, guilt-free nap! Time on retreat often refreshes both body and soul. In fact, some retreat centers offer appointments with a masseuse. At one place, after a nun gave me a wonderful massage, she anointed my hands with oil, praying that God's Spirit would minister through them. Without a heavy schedule and with much time to pray, I find a retreat also provides an ideal time to fast.

In the afternoon or evening, I may browse through the library, find a spot outside, or curl up in a cozy chair to read.

How ever I may spend those precious days or hours, I seek always to be open to the Spirit of God. Most importantly, taking a personal spiritual retreat enables us to enjoy undistracted time with our First Love.

Though going on retreat takes time, effort, and a bit of courage, ironically all those things that scream for my attention before leaving lose their grip on me while I'm away. I often return to my responsibilities with fresh perspective, greater discernment of *His* priorities for me, and strength to do what He calls me to.

How do I locate a retreat center?

To find a retreat center, I suggest calling any Protestant or Catholic church in your area to ask for recommendations. (The majority of retreat centers I have found tend to be Catholic but welcome people from any denomination. Also, many monasteries are open to female retreatants, and abbeys to male.) A helpful resource available at libraries and bookstores is *Sanctuaries: The Complete United States: A Guide to Lodgings in Monasteries, Abbeys, and Retreats*, by Jack and Marcia Kelly. Additional guides under the same title, but specific to the Northeast, the West Coast and the Southwest have been published. Also, Retreats International publishes an annual Directory of Retreats in the United States and Canada (for a cost of $25, call 1–800–556–4532).

What does it cost?

Many retreat centers charge a suggested donation based upon whether or not food is included and upon the location of the retreat center. (The costs usually range from $20–65 a night.) Most also offer scholarships or help with the cost if needed (or they simply ask you to pay what you can afford).

HARD OF HEARING

> O Lord, it has been a long time
> since I have sat at your feet . . .
> since my heart has wept at the words of your Spirit,
> the wonder of your grace.
> My ears have grown dull to your whispers of love,
> whispers of conviction,
> whispers of hope.
> Though young in years,
> I have become hard of hearing.
> *"If only my people would listen to Me,"* You cry.
> *"Hear, you deaf!"* You shout.
> How I am like those stubborn Israelites—
> the ones at whom I often shake my head.
> To them and to me, You say,
> You have seen many things, *but you do not observe them;*
> Your ears are open, but none hears.

I plan and work and strive;
yet, my heart petrifies as I dwell in the
shelter of self-reliance.
Break forth, O Lord, in shouts of love
and rupture the corroded membrane that dulls
the ears of my heart.
Silence the fretful noise in my mind
which drowns out Your still small voice.
Draw me, like Mary, to Your Self,
to pour upon Your feet that which I hold most precious
in the alabaster vial of my heart.
Call me, like Mary, to sit and wait in silence,
to listen to your words of tenderness and love.
Then lift me up, Lord, into Your arms
and place in me a new heart and
a new spirit as you promise:
a heart that hears, a spirit that responds.

"And I shall take the heart of stone out of their flesh and give them a heart of flesh, that they may walk in My statutes and keep My ordinances, and do them. Then they will be My people, and I shall be their God" (Ezekiel 11:19–20).

MYSTERY OF DESIRE

HOW TO PRAY ABOUT UNFULFILLED LONGINGS[3]

When we face the ache of unfulfilled longings, at times we may find it difficult to know how to pray. Here are some suggestions to help:

1. Be real with God. Like David, we can pour out our hearts before God (Psalm 62:8). Be honest with Him about all your desires—even those you may feel ashamed of. He knows them anyway. Lay them at His feet.

2. Pray for passion for Christ. Pray that God will turn your passion for your desires into fuel stoking your passion for Him.

Ask Him to help you see the desire for Him underneath all your desires.

David prayed, "One thing I have asked from the LORD, that I shall seek: that I may dwell in the house of the LORD all the days of my life, to behold the beauty of the LORD, and to meditate in His temple" (Psalm 27:4). Pray to seek, like David, to dwell in His house.

3. Ask God to purify your desires and devotion. Paul writes, "I am afraid, lest as the serpent deceived Eve by his craftiness, your minds be led astray from the simplicity and purity of devotion to Christ" (2 Corinthians 11:3). Be on guard for the deceiver's tactics to stir up desires that distract your devotion to God.

4. "Delight yourself in the LORD, and He will give you the desires of your heart" (Psalm 37:4). Ask God to write *His* desires upon your heart so that you desire what He desires for you. Ask Him to help you believe that His desires for you are far better and more satisfying than yours could ever be.

5. Pray for a thankful and content heart with all that is currently yours: "Be content with what you have" (Hebrews 13:5 NIV). When I list the many blessings in my life—family, friends, the ability to work, the ability to move and breathe and see and taste, a home, a clear mind—I feel incredibly blessed and full.

6. Ask God to grant you a greater sense of eternity and of the temporariness of this life. "We look not at the things which are seen, but at the things which are not seen; for the things which are seen are temporal, but the things which are not seen are eternal" (2 Corinthians 4:18).

Pray for an eternal perspective on your life and a longing for heaven, our real home. A friend in a letter observed, "It has been said that we may be the first generation of people that expect to find fulfillment in the present life. We don't look forward to eternity."

7. Close your times of prayer with praise and meditation.

Praise—that God is able to do exceedingly abundantly beyond all that we ask or imagine; praise that He is good and full of lovingkindness and compassion; that a wonderful inheritance awaits us.

Meditate—on His Word and promises such as, "The LORD is my Shepherd; I have everything I need" (Psalm 23:1 NLT); "My God shall supply all your needs according to His riches" (Philippians 4:19); or whatever verses quiet your heart about your longings.

MYSTERY OF HOPE

"Life for the Chrisian is, on one level, no different than for anybody else who treads this earth. We breathe the same air, look up at the same night sky, wear the same clothes, work at the same sort of jobs, have the same aspirations for love and family, face the same trials and tribulations, and on and on.

"The difference is, we who have answered the call to come home to God, while certainly no better than anybody else nor more free from our share of life's disasters, do not walk the pilgrim way alone. One is with us who will never leave our side nor end his watch over us."

—Eugene Peterson, *A Long Obedience in the Same Direction*

MYSTERY OF DELIGHT

Love bade me welcome; yet my soul drew back,
Guilty of dust and sin.
But quick-eyed Love, observing me grow slack
From my first entrance in,
Drew nearer to me, sweetly questioning,
If I lacked anything.
A guest, I answered, worthy to be here:
Love said, You shall be he.
I the unkind, ungrateful? Ah my dear,
I cannot look on thee.

Love took my hand, and smiling did reply,
Who made the eyes but I?
Truth Lord, but I have marred them, let my shame
Go where it doth deserve.
And know you not, says Love, who bore the blame?
My dear, then I will serve.
You must sit down, says Love, and taste my meat:
So I did sit and eat.
　　　—George Herbert, seventeenth-century English poet
　　　and clergyman, "Love" (III)

"Fellowship with God is delightful beyond all telling. He communes with His redeemed ones in an easy, uninhibited fellowship that is restful and healing to the soul. He is not sensitive nor selfish nor temperamental. What He is today we shall find Him tomorrow and the next day and the next year. He is not hard to please, though He may be hard to satisfy. He expects of us only what He has Himself first supplied.

"How good it would be if we could learn that God is easy to live with. He remembers our frame and knows that we are but dust. He may sometimes chasten us, it is true, but even this He does with a smile, the proud, tender smile of a Father who is bursting with pleasure over an imperfect but promising son who is coming every day to look more and more like the One whose child he is.

"We please Him most not by frantically trying to make ourselves good, but by throwing ourselves into His arms with all our imperfections, and believing that he understands everything and loves us still."

　　　　　　　　　　　　　　　　　　—A. W. Tozer

MYSTERY OF LIFE

"Listen to your life. Touch, taste, smell your way to the holy hidden heart of it because all moments are key moments and life itself is grace."

　　　　　　　　　—Frederick Buechner, *Now and Then*

"I simply believe that there is a mystery of the ordinary, that the commonplace is full of wonder, and that this life that we call Christian is different from what we think it is. It is infinitely more subtle, more powerful, more dangerous, more magnificent, more exciting, more humorous, more delicious, more adventurous, more involved, and more troublesome than most of us think. Through Christ each of us is capable of an almost unbounded courage of compassion, and that to live fully this life that God has given us, no matter what circumstances may be, can be a rare and ennobling experience."

—Tim Hansel, *You Gotta Keep Dancing*

"I would rather be a superb meteor, every atom of me in magnificent glow, than a sleepy and permanent planet. The proper function of man is to live, not to exist. I shall not waste my days in trying to prolong them. I shall use my time."

—Jack London, novelist

"I get up. I walk. I fall down. Meanwhile, I keep dancing."

—Hillel

"Until one is committed, there is hesitancy, the chance to draw back, always ineffectiveness. Concerning all acts of initiative (and creation), there is one elementary truth, the ignorance of which kills countless ideas and splendid plans: that the moment one definitely commits oneself, then Providence moves too. All sorts of things occur to help one that would never otherwise have occurred. A whole stream of events issues from the decision, raising in one's favor all manner of unforeseen incidents and meetings and material assistance, which no man could have dreamt would have come his way. I have learned a deep respect for one of Goethe's couplets:

Whatever you can do, or dream you can, begin it.
Boldness has genius, power, and magic in it."

—W. H. Murray

BIBLIOGRAPHY

Barnes, Craig. *Yearning: Living Between How It Is and How It Ought to Be.* Downers Grove, Ill.: InterVarsity Press, 1991.

Becknell, Thomas, and Mary Ellen Ashcroft, eds. *The Beginning of Wisdom: Prayers for Growth and Understanding.* Nashville: Moorings, 1995.

Blomquist, Jean. *Wrestling Till Dawn: Awakening to Life in Times of Struggle.* Nashville: Upper Room, 1994.

Brother Lawrence. *The Practice of the Presence of God.* Mt. Vernon, N.Y.: Peter Pauper Press, 1963.

Brussat, Frederic, and Mary Ann. *Spiritual Literacy: Reading the Sacred in Everyday Life.* New York: Scribner and Sons, 1996.

Buber, Martin. *The Way of Man.* New York: Citadel Press, 1966.

Buechner, Frederick. *Wishful Thinking: A Theological ABC.* New York: Harper & Row, 1973.

———. *The Magnificent Defeat.* San Francisco: Harper & Row, 1966.

Chesterton, G. K. *Orthodoxy.* Wheaton, Ill.: Harold Shaw Publishers, 1994.

Foster, Richard. *Celebration of Discipline.* New York: Harper & Row, 1978.

Gateley, Edwina. *Psalms of a Laywoman*. Franklin, Wis.: Sheed & Ward, 1981.

Gire, Ken. *The Reflective Life: Becoming More Spiritually Sensitive to the Everyday Moments of Life*. Colorado Springs: Chariot Victor, 1998.

Guyon, Mme. Jeanne. *Final Steps in Christian Maturity*. Sargent, Ga.: Christian Books, 1985.

Hansel, Tim. *You Gotta Keep Dancing: In the Midst of Life's Hurts, You Can Choose Joy!* Elgin, Ill.: David C. Cook Publishing, 1985.

———. *When I Relax I Feel Guilty*. Elgin, Ill.: David C. Cook Publishing, 1979.

Hazard, David, ed. *I Promise You a Crown: A 40-Day Journey in the Company of Julian of Norwich*. Minneapolis: Bethany House Publishers, 1995.

Hurnard, Hannah. *The Hearing Heart*. Wheaton, Ill.: Tyndale House, 1981.

———. *Hind's Feet on High Places*. Wheaton, Ill.: Tyndale House, 1977.

Job, Reuben, and Norman Shawchuck. *A Guide to Prayer for Ministers and Other Servants*. Nashville: The Upper Room, 1983.

Lamott, Anne. *Traveling Mercies: Some Thoughts on Faith*. New York: Anchor Books, 1999.

Laubach, Frank, and Brother Lawrence. *Practicing His Presence*. Sargent, Ga.: The Seed Sowers, 1973.

L'Engle, Madeleine. *Walking on Water: Reflections on Faith and Art*. Wheaton, Ill.: Harold Shaw Publishers, 1998.

Lewis, C. S. CHRONICLES OF NARNIA: *The Lion, the Witch and the Wardrobe*. New York: HarperCollins Publishers, 1978.

———. CHRONICLES OF NARNIA: *The Silver Chair*. New York: HarperCollins Publishers, 1978.

———. *Letters to an American Lady*. Grand Rapids, Mich.: Eerdmans, 1967.

———. *Letters to Malcolm, Chiefly on Prayer*. New York: Harcourt, Brace & World Inc., 1964.

———. *Mere Christianity*. New York: Macmillan, 1952.

———. *The Problem of Pain*. New York: Macmillan, 1962.

———. *Screwtape Letters*. New York: Macmillan, 1976.

———. *The Weight of Glory and Other Addresses*. New York: Macmillan, 1962.

Llewelyn, Robert. *Daily Readings With Julian of Norwich*. Springfield, Ill.: Templegate Publication, 1980.

Manning, Brennan. *Abba's Child: The Cry of the Heart for Intimate Belonging*. Colorado Springs: NavPress, 1994.

Marshall, Catherine. *To Live Again*. Grand Rapids, Mich.: Chosen Books, 1996.

Merton, Thomas. *No Man Is an Island*. Garden City, N.Y.: Image Books, 1967.

Mother Teresa. *Everything Starts From Prayer*. Ashland, Ore.: White Cloud Press, 1998.

Norris, Kathleen. *Amazing Grace: A Vocabulary of Faith*. New York: Riverhead Books, 1998.

———. *The Cloister Walk*. New York: Riverhead Books, 1996.

Nouwen, Henri. *Genessee Diary*. New York: Bantam Doubleday Dell, 1976.

———. *Inner Voice of Love*. New York: Bantam Doubleday Dell, 1996.

———. *Life of the Beloved*. New York: CrossRoad Publishing, 1992.

———. *Making All things New: An Invitation to the Spiritual Life*. San Francisco: Harper & Row, 1981.

———. *Out of Solitude*. South Bend, Ind.: Ave Maria Press, 1974.

———. *Return of the Prodigal Son*. New York: Bantam Doubleday Dell, 1992.

Obbard, Elizabeth Ruth. *Magnificant: The Journey and the Song*. London: Darton, Longman and Todd, 1985.

Packer, J. I. *Knowing God*. Downers Grove, Ill.: InterVarsity Press, 1973.

Peterson, Eugene H. *The Contemplative Pastor: Returning to the Art of Spiritual Direction*. Grand Rapids, Mich.: Eerdmans, 1989.

———. *Psalms*. Colorado Springs: NavPress Publishing Group, 1995.

————. *The Message: The New Testament in Contemporary Language.* Colorado Springs: NavPress, 1993.

Piper, John. *The Pleasures of God.* Portland, Ore.: Multnomah Press, 1991.

————. *Desiring God.* Portland, Ore.: Multnomah Press, 1986.

Rhodes, Tricia McCary. *The Soul at Rest.* Minneapolis: Bethany House, 1996.

Rilke, Ranier Maria. *Letters to a Young Poet,* rev. ed. Trans., M. D. Herter Norton. New York: W. W. Norton & Co., 1954.

Rubietta, Jane. *Quiet Places: A Woman's Guide to Personal Retreat.* Minneapolis: Bethany House, 1997.

Rupp, Joyce. *May I Have this Dance?* Notre Dame, Ind.: Ave Maria Press, 1992.

Steindl-Rast, David. *The Music of Silence.* San Francisco: Harper & Row, 1995.

Thomas à Kempis. *The Imitation of Christ.* Springdale, Pa.: Whitaker House, 1981.

Thomas, Gary. *Sacred Marriage.* Grand Rapids, Mich.: Zondervan, 2000.

————. *The Glorious Pursuit: Embracing the Virtues of Christ.* Colorado Springs: NavPress, 1998.

Tozer, A. W. *The Knowledge of the Holy.* New York: Harper & Row, 1961.

————. *The Pursuit of God: The Human Thirst for the Divine.* Camp Hill, Pa.: Christian Publications, 1982.

Trobisch, Walter. *I Married You.* New York: Harper & Row, 1971.

Trueblood, D. Elton. *The Common Ventures of Life: Marriage, Birth, Work, Death.* New York: Harper & Brothers, 1949.

Vanauken, Sheldon. *A Severe Mercy.* New York: Bantam Books, 1977.

White, John, *Daring to Draw Near.* Madison, Wis.: InterVarsity Press, 1977.

Willard, Dallas. *The Spirit of the Disciplines.* New York: HarperCollins Publishers, 1991.

ENDNOTES

INTRODUCTION

1. For an in-depth guide to scriptural meditation, see Tricia McCary Rhodes, *The Soul at Rest* (Minneapolis: Bethany House, 1996).

CHAPTER ONE

1. L. M. Boyd, "Child's Play Everywhere Includes Hide-and-Seek," *San Francisco Chronicle*, n.d., B3.
2. BeBe Winans, "All of Me," *My Utmost for His Highest: The Covenant* CD, O'Ryan Music/Word Music, 1996.
3. A. W. Tozer, *The Pursuit of God: The Human Thirst for the Divine* (Camp Hill, Pa: Christian Publications), 63.
4. Martin Buber, *The Way of Man* (New York: Citadel Press, 1966), 12 (italics added).
5. Brennan Manning, *Abba's Child: The Cry of the Heart for Intimate Belonging* (Colorado Springs: NavPress, 1994), 90.
6. Ibid, 50.
7. Buber, 16–17.

CHAPTER TWO

1. Frederic and Mary Ann Brussat, *Spiritual Literacy: Reading the Sacred in Everyday Life* (New York: Scribner and Sons, 1996), 419.
2. Frederick Buechner, *Wishful Thinking: A Theological ABC* (New York: Harper & Row, 1973), 53–54.
3. C. S. Lewis, *Mere Christianity* (New York: Macmillan, 1952), 99.
4. Elizabeth Ruth Obbard, *Magnificat: The Journey and the Song* (London: Darton, Longman, and Todd, 1985), 35.
5. Brussat, 419.
6. Buechner, 85.

CHAPTER THREE

1. Henri Nouwen, *Life of the Beloved* (New York: CrossRoad Publishing, 1992), 75.
2. Anne Lamott, *Traveling Mercies: Some Thoughts on Faith* (New York: Anchor Books, 1999), 68.
3. Obbard, 40.
4. Donna Hatasaki, "Remembering Jennifer and Jessica," *Young Life Relationships*, Spring/Summer 2000, 17.

CHAPTER FOUR

1. Nouwen, 90.
2. Craig Barnes, *Yearning* (Downers Grove, Ill.: InterVarsity Press, 1991), 31.

CHAPTER FIVE

1. Portions of this chapter have been adapted from Stacey S. Padrick, "Five Myths About Suffering," *Discipleship Journal*, issue 113, Sept/Oct 1999.
2. Hannah Hurnard, *Hind's Feet on High Places* (Wheaton, Ill.: Tyndale House, 1977), 66, 232.
3. Mrs. Charles E. Cowman, ed. *Streams in the Desert*, vol. 1 (Grand Rapids, Mich: Zondervan, 1997), 61.
4. Dale Hanson Bourke, "Should We Be Glad for How Little We Suffer?" Syndicated column.
5. Joel Green, *The Way of the Cross* (Nashville: Discipleship Resources, 1988), 42.

6. Thomas à Kempis, *The Imitation of Christ* (Springdale, Pa.: Whitaker House, 1981) 83–84.
7. Craig Brian Larson, "The Power of Positive and Negative Preaching," *Leadership Journal*, Winter 1995, 81.
8. A. W. Tozer, *The Knowledge of the Holy* (New York: Harper & Row, 1961), 69–70.

CHAPTER SIX

1. Henri J. M. Nouwen, *Out of Solitude* (South Bend, Ind.: Ave Maria Press, 1974), 14.
2. Ibid., 21–22.
3. John Leax, *Grace Is Where I Live: Writing As a Christian Vocation* (Grand Rapids, Mich.,: Baker Books, 1993), 49.
4. Tozer, *The Pursuit of God*, 75–76.
5. Mme. Jeanne Guyon, *Final Steps in Christian Maturity* (Sargent, Ga.: Christian Books, 1985), 7.
6. Thomas Merton, *No Man Is an Island* (Garden City, N.Y.: Image Books, 1967), 194.
7. Thomas Kelly, c. 1941, *Daily Readings From Quaker Writings: Ancient and Modern*, ed., Linda Hill Renfer (Grant's Pass, Ore.: Serenity Press, 1988), 365.

CHAPTER SEVEN

1. Tozer, *The Pursuit of God*, 17.
2. Thomas à Kempis, 126.
3. Augustine, *Confessions*, 24, ii [2] (emphasis added).
4. John Piper, *Desiring God: Meditations from a Christian Hedonist* (Sisters, Ore.: Multnomah Press, 1986), 55.
5. C. S. Lewis, *The Silver Chair*, from THE CHRONICLES OF NARNIA (New York: HarperCollins Publishers, 1978).
6. Tozer, *The Pursuit of God*, 40.
7. Manning, 51.
8. Adapted from *Reflections of God's Glory*; reprinted in "A Legacy Continues," *TransWorld Radio Magazine*, vol. 20, issue 1, 16.

CHAPTER EIGHT

1. Barnes, 21.
2. David Hazard, ed., *I Promise You a Crown: A 40-Day Journey in the*

Company of Julian of Norwich (Minneapolis: Bethany House Publishers, 1995), 40.

CHAPTER NINE

1. C. S. Lewis, *The Problem of Pain* (New York: Macmillan, 1962), 46–47.
2. Tozer, *The Pursuit of God*, 32.
3. Augustine, 13, xxxi [300].
4. C. S. Lewis, *Screwtape Letters* (New York: Macmillan, 1976), 106.
5. Madeleine L'Engle, *Walking on Water: Reflections on Faith and Art* (Wheaton, Ill.: Harold Shaw Publishers, 1998), 73.
6. Nouwen, *Life of the Beloved*, 31.

CHAPTER TEN

1. Maya Angelou, *Wouldn't Take Nothing for My Journey Now*, quoted in Brussat, *Spiritual Literacy*, 466 (emphasis added).
2. C. S. Lewis, *The Lion, the Witch, and the Wardrobe*, from THE CHRONICLES OF NARNIA (New York: HarperCollins Publishers, 1950), 86.
3. Oswald Chambers, *My Utmost for His Highest*, from the reading for October 10.
4. Tim Hansel, *You Gotta Keep Dancing: In the Midst of Life's Hurts, You Can Choose Joy!* (Elgin, Ill.: Cook Publishing, 1985), 38.

EPILOGUE

1. Stacey S. Padrick, previously published in *Discipleship Journal* as "How Can I Pray in the Midst of Darkness?" issue 113, Sept/Oct 1999, 28.
2. Partially adapted from an article by Stacey S. Padrick published in *Discipleship Journal* as "Rendezvous With God," issue 120, Nov/Dec 2000, 30–35.
3. Stacey S. Padrick, to be printed in *Discipleship Journal*, Nov/Dec 2001.

Thank you for selecting a book from
BETHANY HOUSE PUBLISHERS

Bethany House Publishers is a ministry of Bethany Fellowship
International, an interdenominational, nonprofit organization
committed to spreading the Good News of Jesus Christ around
the world through evangelism, church planting, literature
distribution, and care for those in need. Missionary training is
offered through Bethany College of Missions.

Bethany Fellowship International is a member of the National
Association of Evangelicals and subscribes to its statement of
faith. If you would like further information, please contact:

Bethany Fellowship International
6820 Auto Club Road
Bloomington, MN 55438 USA